**"Let's spend the night t...
Luke said eve...
morning I'll ...
airport and w...
ways."**

Katrin's lashes flickered. "Without any emotions, is that what you mean?"

"Without us getting entangled in a relationship neither of us wants."

"You have it all figured out."

"You can say no, Katrin," Luke reminded her in a hard voice.

Katrin glared at him, tilting her chin. "I'm not going to do that."

"So is that a resounding yes?"

"You don't want a resounding anything!"

"At least I'm honest about it. So what will it be, Katrin? Yes or no?"

Anything can happen behind closed doors!

Do you dare to find out...?

Welcome again to DO NOT DISTURB!

Luke McRae is a man used to getting his own way, both in the boardroom and in the bedroom. But then he meets Katrin, a beautiful woman also used to living life on her terms. Together they make a deal to share a bed, but soon discover that they definitely *don't* want to be disturbed!

Join Presents® author Sandra Field for a ride on a unique journey to love, one that you simply won't want to put down.

So what happens when Katrin becomes Luke's mistress for one night of unrelenting passion?

Turn the pages and find out!

Sandra Field

ON THE TYCOON'S TERMS

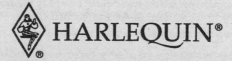

TORONTO • NEW YORK • LONDON
AMSTERDAM • PARIS • SYDNEY • HAMBURG
STOCKHOLM • ATHENS • TOKYO • MILAN • MADRID
PRAGUE • WARSAW • BUDAPEST • AUCKLAND

ISBN 0-373-12348-5

ON THE TYCOON'S TERMS

First North American Publication 2003.

Printed in U.S.A.

CHAPTER ONE

"LUKE! Good to see you, did you just arrive?"

"Hi there, John," Luke MacRae said, shaking the older man's hand. "Got in an hour ago. Jet-lagged, as usual." And remarkably reluctant to be here, he added to himself although he had no intentions of telling John that. "How about yourself?"

"Earlier in the day.... There's someone here I'd like you to meet, he's got some holdings in Malaysia that might interest you."

"Inland?" Luke asked, and to his satisfaction heard the slight edge to his voice, the intentness that had brought him to where he was today: owner of a worldwide mining conglomerate. He and John were two of the delegates at an international conference on mining being held at a resort beside one of Manitoba's vast lakes.

"You'll have to ask him the exact location." John signaled to the nearest waitress. "What'll you have, Luke?"

"Scotch on the rocks," Luke said crisply, sparing a moment to wonder why the waitress was wearing such ugly glasses. She might be rather pretty without them.

He was deep in conversation with the Malaysian, who did indeed interest him, when an exquisitely modulated voice to his left said, "Your drink, sir."

The voice didn't in the least match the dark-framed glasses or the blond hair strained back under a frilly white cap. Uptight about her femininity and deadly dull into the bargain, Luke decided. Despite that very intriguing voice.

It was a game of his to make instant assessments of people; he was very rarely wrong. One thing was certain. The waitress wasn't the kind of woman who turned his crank. "Thanks," he said briefly, then forgot her right away.

Three-quarters of an hour later they all moved into the dining room; his table, he noticed automatically, had the best location as far as the view of the lake was concerned, and its occupants were the real powers behind this conference. He had long ago trained himself not to feel any self-satisfaction from such arrangements. He was good. He knew it and didn't dwell on it. Power for the sake of power had never interested him.

Power was security. Security against the kind of childhood he'd had.

Luke took his seat, running his fingers around his collar. Dammit, he never thought about his childhood. Just because Teal Lake, where he'd been born, was in nearby northern Ontario was no reason to indulge in maudlin memories. The proximity of his old home was, of course, the reason he was reluctant to be here. Although *home* was the laugh of the century. Neither of his parents had provided him with much of a home in the little mining town of Teal Lake.

Quickly Luke picked up the leather-bound menu and made his choices; then his eyes flicked over the other occupants of the table.

The only surprise was sitting directly across from him: Guy Wharton. Inherited money without the requisite brains to manage it had been Luke's opinion of Guy the first time he'd met him, and any subsequent encounters hadn't caused him to change his mind. Unfortunately Guy's wealth was coupled with a tendency to throw his weight around.

The bartender took their orders, then the waitress started at the other end of the table. The waitress with the glasses and the beautiful voice, Luke thought idly. Guy had brought his drink to the table, and was now ordering a double, as well as a bottle of very good wine that would be wasted on him. Guy drinking was several steps worse than Guy sober. Luke turned his attention to his neighbor, a charming Englishman with an unerring nose for the commodity market; then heard that smooth contralto voice again. "Sir? May I take your order?"

"I'll have smoked salmon and the rack of lamb, medium rare," Luke said. She nodded politely, then addressed his companion. She wasn't writing anything down; her eyes behind the overlarge lenses, he saw with a little jolt, were a clear, intelligent blue. Not dull at all. Somehow Luke was quite sure she'd keep all the orders straight.

Well, of course she'd be good at her job; a resort like this wouldn't hire duds.

Waitresses and Teal Lake…he was losing it. "Rupert," he asked, "what are your thoughts on silver over the next couple of months?"

The Englishman launched into a highly technical assessment, to which Luke paid close attention. Wine was poured into his glass; he sipped it sparingly, noticing that Guy's face was already flushed and his voice overloud. The smoked salmon was excellent; the rack of lamb tender and the vegetables crisp. Then Luke noticed Guy signaling the waitress. She came instantly, her severe black uniform with its white apron effectively hiding her figure. But nothing could hide a certain pride of bearing, Luke thought slowly; although she wasn't a tall woman, she walked tall, like someone who knew who she was and liked herself. Yet he'd categorized her as deadly dull…was he going to prove himself wrong for once?

"The steak," Guy said loudly. "I asked for medium. You brought rare."

"I'm so sorry, sir," she said. "I'll take it back to the kitchen and bring one more to your liking."

But as she reached down for his plate, Guy grabbed her

by the wrist. "Why didn't you do it right the first time? You're being paid to bring me what I ask for."

"Yes, sir," she said. "If you'll let go, I'll make sure your steak is brought to you immediately."

There were faint pink patches in her cheeks; her mouth, Luke noticed, was set, her whole body rigid. But Guy didn't let go. Instead he twisted her wrist, leering up at her. "You should take those stupid glasses off," he said. "No man in his right mind'll look at you with those on."

"Please let go of my wrist."

This time, she hadn't said *sir.* Without stopping to think, Luke pushed himself partway up from his chair and said in a voice like a steel blade, "Guy, you heard the lady. Let go of her. Now," and noticed from the corner of his eye the maître d' heading toward their table.

"Only kidding," Guy said, running his fingers over the woman's palm, then releasing her wrist with deliberate slowness. The waitress didn't even glance at Luke as she quickly removed Guy's plate and hurried away from the table.

"I didn't find it funny," Luke said coldly. "Nor, I'm sure, did anyone else. Including her."

"For Pete's sake, she's just a waitress. And we all know what they're after."

Luke was quite sure the waitress with the ugly glasses wasn't after anyone. If she were, she'd wear contacts, and make the most of eyes that could be truly startling were they not framed by thick plastic. Pointedly he turned to the man on his other side, an Italian goldminer. A few minutes later the maître d' brought Guy another plate. "Please let me know if that's not to your satisfaction, sir," he said with meticulous politeness.

"She chickened out, did she?" Guy smirked.

"I beg your pardon, sir?"

"You heard," Guy said. "Yeah, this is okay."

Brandishing his knife as he talked, he began telling an off-color story to his neighbor.

When they'd finished their entrées, it was the waitress who removed their plates. Her name tag said Katrin. Luke had read that the resort was near a village that had been settled over a hundred years ago by Icelandic immigrants; with her blond hair and blue eyes, she certainly fit the stereotype. Then, as she reached for his plate, he saw on her wrist the red mark where Guy had twisted her skin, and felt an upsurge of rage that was out of all proportion.

Because he'd always loathed men who picked on those who were weaker, or otherwise powerless to defend themselves? Because basic justice was a tenet he held no matter what the class distinctions?

He said nothing; the woman had already made it all too clear she hadn't been grateful for his intervention. In no mood for dessert, he ordered a coffee.

"Join me in a brandy?" John murmured.

"No, thanks," Luke replied. "Jet lag's catching up on me, I'm going to call it a day very shortly."

This was true enough. But Luke had never been one for alcoholic excess; his father had drunk enough for five men. One more reason why Guy's drunken pronouncements had gotten under his skin. He and John talked briefly about the abysmal markets for copper and nickel; then Luke saw Katrin approaching their table with a loaded tray of rich desserts. She lowered it skilfully onto the dumbwaiter and started distributing tortes and cheesecakes with scarcely a pause. She had a very good memory and was extraordinarily efficient, he thought with reluctant admiration. So what else had he missed in his initial assessment?

Guy had ordered a double brandy. As she started to put it on the table, he deliberately brushed his arm against her breast. "Mmm...nice," he sneered. "You hiding anything else under that uniform?"

So quickly he wondered if he'd imagined it, Luke saw a flash of blue fire behind her ludicrous glasses. Then the brandy snifter tipped as though the stem had slipped through her fingers. The contents drenched Guy's sleeve and trickled down his pale blue shirt. "Oh, sir," she exclaimed, "how careless of me. Let me get you a napkin."

As Guy surged to his feet, his face mottled with rage, Luke also stood up. She'd done it on purpose, he thought, and suppressed a quiver of true amusement: the kind he rarely felt. "Guy," he said softly, "you cause any more trouble at this table, and I personally will see that the deal you're working on with Amco Steel gets shelved. Permanently. Do you hear me?"

There was a small, deadly silence. Guy wanted that deal, everyone at the table knew that. Wanted it very badly. Guy snarled, "You're a bastard, MacRae."

Technically Guy was telling the exact truth: Luke's father had never bothered marrying Luke's mother. But Luke had long ago buried any feelings around the circumstances of his birth. "I'll kill the deal before it even gets to the table," he said. "Now sit down and behave yourself."

Katrin had reached for a serviette from the shelf below the dumbwaiter. As she straightened, she gave Luke a withering look which said more clearly than words that she neither needed nor appreciated his help, and passed the crisply folded linen to Guy. "The resort will, of course, look after the dry cleaning of your suit, sir," she said, and very calmly passed out the remainder of the drinks and desserts, as if nothing had happened.

Adding a formidable self-control to his list of the shapeless and bespectacled Katrin's qualities, Luke drained his coffee cup and said flatly, "Good night, all. According to my time zone it's 2:00 a.m., and I'm going to hit the pit. See you all in the morning."

On the way out, he stopped to speak briefly to the maître d'.

"I trust there'll be no repercussions for the waitress at our table," he said. "If he were working in my office, Mr. Wharton would be slapped with a sexual harassment charge. And I'd make damn sure it stuck."

The maître d', who was at least five years younger than Luke's thirty-three, said noncommittally, "Thank you, sir."

"I'm sure there'll be no further trouble from Mr. Wharton."

"Certainly, sir."

Luke said pleasantly, "If she's fired or otherwise penalized, I'll file a complaint with the management."

"That won't be necessary, sir."

Suddenly Luke was tired of the whole game. Why was he wasting his time on a woman who patently couldn't care less about him, and had resented his help? Bed, that was where he should be, he decided, and marched toward the elevators.

In bed. Alone. As he'd been for rather too long.

Once he got back to San Francisco, he must do something about that.

CHAPTER TWO

LUKE slept well, went for an early morning run, then returned to his room to shower and dress. After straightening his discreet silk tie, he shrugged into a jacket and ran a comb through his black hair; he'd had it trimmed last week in Milan, although nothing could subdue its tendency to curl. He glanced quickly in the mirror, meeting his own dark brown eyes, so dark as to be almost black. He'd do. He looked his usual self: well-groomed, single-minded and totally in control.

Not bad for a kid from Teal Lake.

Luke grimaced irritably. He didn't want to think about Teal Lake. Now or ever. So why was he standing here admiring himself when he should be downstairs? There were some valuable contacts he could cement in the next few days.

He took the elevator to the main floor. The resort might be situated in the wilderness but there was nothing remotely backwoods about it. The dining room had tall, velvet-draped windows and a magnificent stone fireplace, flanked by striking oil paintings of the prairie wheatfields. It was mid-July, the lake as smooth as the mirror in his room, the eastern sky a limpid blue.

He'd like to be out there, Luke thought. Capturing the sky's serenity with his digital camera.

But not right now; there were more important things to do. As he started across the room to his table, Katrin the waitress emerged from the kitchen. She was wearing a peasant skirt and an embroidered blouse. He said cheerfully, "Good morning, Katrin."

12

Her steps didn't even falter. "Good morning, sir."

In three words she managed to imply that although being polite to him was part of her job, it was far from her personal preference. Again Luke felt that wayward flash of true amusement. He'd been insulted many times in his life, both as a raw kid working the mines of the Arctic and as a ruthless entrepreneur. But rarely with such finesse. Not one wasted word.

He'd like to pluck those god-awful glasses off her nose.

He'd reached his table. Guy was noticeable by his absence. No loss, thought Luke, and sat down so that his back was to the lake. He didn't want to look at water. He had work to do.

And work he did, all day. Lunch was served buffet-style in the foyer to the conference rooms; Katrin was nowhere to be seen. Before dinner, Luke went to the fully equipped exercise room to get rid of the pressures of the day. On the whole, he was pleased with the way things were going. He had Malaysia hooked; and could feel himself backing off from a strip mine in Papua New Guinea. Long ago he'd learned to trust his instincts, and they were all screaming beware. Labor troubles, gangsters and environmental destruction: not his cup of tea.

An hour later, feeling both relaxed and alert, Luke was crossing the lobby toward the dining room. A smartly dressed woman walking in the opposite direction gave him an assessing glance, followed by a smile that was rather more than casual. Luke was used to this; it happened to him all the time. His own smile back was courteous, nothing more.

As he waited for the maître d', he wondered idly what it was about him that attracted women. His suit and shirt were custom-tailored, his shoes Italian; both outward signs of wealth. But lots of other men were similarly garbed. So it wasn't just his money. He wasn't blind to his height, his athletic build and the regularity of his features; and had always assumed that they were what drew women to him. What he was unaware of was his aura of decisiveness, of hard-won power, of sheer male energy and banked sexuality; unaware also of the impact of his rare smile, that softened his deep-set, enigmatic eyes and the hewn masculinity of his jaw.

He was the last to arrive at his table. Katrin was once again wearing her unflattering black uniform; for the first time, Luke noticed how thick the bundle of straight blond hair was under her cap. Loose, it would fall past her shoulders...he suddenly realized she was speaking to him. "What can I get you to drink, sir?"

"Rye and water, no ice, please."

"Certainly, sir."

At what point did politeness turn to parody, he wondered; and decided Katrin knew that point precisely, and wasn't above using it. He sat down.

No one else had noticed anything; perhaps his imagination was working overtime. The odd thing was that, elusively, she reminded him of someone; he'd figured this out while he was doing his routine of bench presses. He'd already searched through all the old Teal Lake contacts, and knew she didn't belong there. So where else could he have met her? Nowhere that he could think of. And yet something about the tilt of her chin, her carriage, set off signals in his brain.

Once again the food was excellent; once again Guy was gulping a fine Shiraz as though it were water and eating Châteaubriand with the appreciation hamburger deserved.

The conversation turned to the vagaries of the stock market. Guy, to do him justice, had one or two insights about insider trading that were worth listening to. As Katrin poured coffee from a sterling pot, moving efficiently from seat to seat, Guy said with overdone bonhomie, "Well,

Katrin, I don't suppose you earn enough to consider investing. But if you did, would you buy into the Alvena bond fund?''

She said woodenly, "I wouldn't know, sir."

"Of course not," Guy said in a voice as smooth as cream. "Let's try something a little closer to your level. How about two-minute portfolios, they're all the rage for people with no smarts who know zilch about the market...is that how you'd invest your money?''

For a split second she hesitated, as though making an inner decision. Then she looked right at Guy, coffeepot suspended, and said crisply, "A two-minute portfolio isn't a bad strategy. When you play the market, you're going to get some duds no matter how careful you are. So by picking from the TSE's top blue-chips, you'll also get enough high-earners to more than offset your losses." She gave him a bland smile. "Would you agree with me, sir?''

Guy flushed an unbecoming brick red. "This coffee tastes like it was brewed yesterday," he snarled.

"I'll make you some fresh, sir," she replied, deftly removing his cup, and with that same unconscious pride of bearing that Luke had noticed the day before, headed for the kitchen.

Luke drawled, "That woman's wasted as a waitress...so what's the prognosis for the S&P over the next six months, Guy?''

For a moment he thought Guy was going to jump across the table at him, and felt all his muscles tighten in anticipation. Then Guy subsided, mumbling something about low percentiles, and the conversation became general again. Luke lingered over a second coffee and was the last to leave the dining room, timing his departure just as Katrin was clearing off a nearby empty table. Soft-footed as a cat, he stepped up behind her. "It'd be a shame if you had to cash in your investments, Katrin," he said, "but you'll lose your job if you go dumping expensive brandy over every customer who insults you.''

She turned to face him, her hands full of dirty wine-glasses, her face expressionless. "I have no idea what you're talking about, sir."

"Last night you spilled brandy all over Guy Wharton on purpose.''

"Why would I do that? Waitresses don't have feelings—they can't afford to."

"Then you're the exception that proves the rule. I wish to God you'd take those glasses off...then I might have some idea what you *are* feeling."

She stepped back in sudden alarm. "My feelings, or lack of them, are none of your business...sir."

She was right, of course. "I also wish you'd stop calling me *sir*."

"It's one of the house rules," she said frigidly. "Another of which is that guests and staff don't fraternize. So if you'll excuse me, sir, I have work to do."

"You're wasted in a job like this, you're far too intelligent."

She said tightly, "My choice of job is just that—*my* choice. Good night, sir."

She had turned away. Short of grabbing her by the arm, a move he had no intention of making, Luke knew the conversation was over. Score: Katrin, one; Luke, zero. He said pleasantly, "If you are investing, steer clear of Scitech—it's going down the tubes. Good night, Katrin."

But, just as he was turning away, he heard himself add, "You know, I have the oddest feeling—you remind me of someone, and I can't think who." He hadn't planned to tell her this. Not before he'd pinned down the memory that was teasing his brain.

Her whole body went still: the stillness of prey faced with a predator. She said so quietly he could hardly hear her, "You're mistaken. You're quite wrong—I've never seen you before in my life."

His senses sharpened. Her shoulders were stiff with tension, the same tension that had underlain her voice. So there *was* something mysterious about her. The ugly glasses were nothing to do with hiding her femininity, and everything to do with another kind of disguise. Katrin didn't want to be recognized because she was other than she appeared. He said, thinking out loud, "Right now I can't pin down where I might have seen you...but I'm sure it'll come to me."

Two of the wineglasses slipped through her fingers. As they fell to the carpet, one hit the table leg, shattering into pieces. With a tiny exclamation of distress, Katrin bent to pick them up.

"Careful," Luke exclaimed, "you could cut yourself."

He grabbed a napkin from the table and knelt beside her, wrapping the shards of glass in the thick linen. Her perfume drifted to his nostrils, something floral and delicate. The red mark on her wrist hadn't completely faded; her veins were blue against her creamy skin, her wrist bones fragile. She said raggedly, "Please go away—I'll clean this up."

Jerkily she reached for a splinter of glass. Blood blossomed from her fingertip; she gave a gasp of pain. Luke said urgently, "Katrin, leave this. Here, stand up."

He seized her by the elbow, pulling her to her feet. Then he gently rested her fingers on his sleeve, probing at the wound. She said breathlessly, "Stop, you're hurting."

"There's glass in it, hold still," he ordered, and as carefully as he could extracted a small shard of glass from the cut. "There, that's better. Is there a first-aid kit in the kitchen?"

A male voice said authoritatively, "What's the trouble here, sir?"

The ubiquitous maître d', thought Luke, and wished the man a hundred miles away. "She's cut her finger," he said with equal authority. "Will you please show me where the first-aid kit is?"

"I'll look after—"

"Now," said Luke, transferring his gaze from Katrin's finger to the young man's face. As Luke had known he would, the young man backed off.

"Certainly, sir. This way, please."

The kitchen was in a state of controlled chaos from having produced gourmet meals for two hundred people. The maître d', whose name tag said Olaf, led Luke to a square box in a secluded corner of the kitchen. "Thanks," Luke said briefly, "I can manage now. Perhaps you could see that the remainder of the glass gets picked up."

Without another word, Olaf left. Katrin tried to tug her hand free, saying with suppressed fury, "Who do you think you are, throwing your weight around like this? Giving everybody orders as if you owned the place. It's only a cut, for heaven's sake—I'm perfectly capable of looking after it myself."

Luke rummaged in the kit. "Here, I'm going to douse it with disinfectant, hold still."

"I don't—ouch!"

"I did warn you," Luke said, giving her a crooked grin as he ripped open a pad of sterile gauze. "There, that's better."

Under the black uniform her chest was rising and falling; her eyes, very close to his, were a brilliant blue. On impulse, Luke reached up and snatched the glasses from her nose, putting them down beside the first-aid kit. His heart skipped a beat, then started a slow, heavy thudding in his chest. She had the most beautiful eyes he'd ever seen.

He'd always thought of blue eyes as being open, unguarded, not potentially secretive as gray eyes could be, or his own dark brown. Once again, he'd been wrong, for Katrin's eyes were so deep a blue he'd never be able to fathom them. Her brows were arched; her cheekbones, which had been hidden by the plastic frames, were exquisite. Even as Luke watched, color mounted in her cheeks, subtle as a rosebud unfolding in summer.

He was still holding her by the hand. As he let his finger drift to rest on the pulse at her wrist, it speeded up, fluttering like a frightened bird's. Had he ever in his life felt anything so intimate as those tiny thrusts against his skin? Had he ever allowed himself to?

He wasn't into intimacy; he'd sworn off it years ago. But right now it was as though a chunk of lead had found a flaw in the bulletproof vest he was wearing and had gone straight for the heart. Hitting him where it hurt the most.

Scarcely knowing what he was saying, Luke muttered, "So you feel it, too."

Her lashes flickered. Yanking her hand free, she cried, "I don't know what you're talking about—I don't feel anything! Please…just go away and leave me alone."

Luke made a huge effort to regain control. A control he was famous—or infamous—for maintaining in any situation and at any cost. His voice sounding almost normal, he said, "I'm going to tape your cut. Then I'll go."

"I can do it!"

She sounded desperate. Desperate to be rid of him. And he was no nearer to pinning her down in his memory than he had been at the dining table. "It'll take ten seconds," he said in a hard voice. "Quit arguing."

"You're sure used to having people do what you say." She raised her chin. "I'm not going to cause a scene in the place where I work, you're not worth it. But get on with it—and then get out."

He stripped the paper lining from a plaster. "You don't sound very grateful."

"I don't feel grateful."

"You've made that plain from the start."

"I can look after myself," she snapped. "I don't need some high-powered business type fancying himself as a knight in shining armor and then trotting up five minutes later to claim his reward. Thanks but no thanks."

Luke felt his own temper rise. "You think I did this so we could have a quickie in the corner of the kitchen?"

"You bet."

"That's not the way I operate!"

"You could have fooled me."

Using every bit of his restraint, Luke taped the bandage over her cut. Then he took three steps backward and said with intentional crudity, "No feeling you up, no kisses behind the refrigerator. And—by the looks of you—no thanks, either."

Scarlet flags of fury stained her cheeks. She reached for her glasses and thrust them back on her nose. "You got that right. I don't thank people who insult me."

Making a very determined effort to get his heart rate and his temper back to normal, Luke said dryly, "I've noticed that already. I'll see you at breakfast, Katrin."

"I can wait."

Suddenly he laughed. "How would I ever have guessed?" Then, before she could respond, he turned on his heel and strode along the narrow aisle between ranks of stainless steel refrigerators. The kitchen door swung shut behind him. He crossed the deserted dining room, took the four flights of stairs to his suite, and slammed the door behind him.

For a man who'd made it a mission in life to keep his distance and his cool, especially with regard to the female portion of the population, he'd made a total fool of himself.

Well done, Luke. Tomorrow, at the breakfast table, you'd better concentrate on eating your cereal and minding your own business. So a waitress has gorgeous eyes. So what?

Gorgeous eyes, obvious intelligence and a fiery temper. As well as a healthy dose of independence.

And who in the world did she remind him of?

CHAPTER THREE

AT 3:00 a.m. Luke woke to the black silence of his bedroom punctuated by the pounding of his heart in his ears. He swung his legs over the side of the bed, breathing hard. He'd had his usual nightmare about Teal Lake, the one where his dad had him slammed against a wall and was brandishing a broken beer bottle in his fist. His mother, as always in these dreams, was nowhere to be seen.

She'd left when he was five.

Stow it, Luke told himself. It's only a dream. And you're thirty-three, not five. But his heartbeat was still thumping like a drum, and he knew from experience that it was useless to try and go back to sleep right away. Getting up, he pulled the drapes open and gazed out over the lake, where a half-moon traced a glittering path from horizon to shore. Teal Lake was a tenth the size of this lake; but the moon had been equally beautiful on Teal Lake, and equally indifferent.

With an exclamation of disgust, Luke picked up a financial magazine from the mahogany coffee table and buried himself in an analyst's prediction of the future of OPEC. At four he went back to bed, sleeping in snatches and finally getting up at five-thirty. He decided to go for a run along the lakeshore. Anything was better than being cooped up in this room until the dining room opened.

The breeze was pleasantly cool, the morning sky a pale, innocent blue. Birds chirped in the willows; he startled two deer on the golf course. Far out on the lake he could hear the low growl of boats: fishermen catching pickerel and goldeye, for which the lake was famous. He must have some for dinner tonight; the goldeye in particular was considered a delicacy. He'd have to ask Katrin her opinion, he thought sardonically. Sure. Good luck.

Pushing himself, Luke jogged for nearly an hour, sweat soaking his hair and gluing his T-shirt to his chest. He started to slow down when he reached the wharf that was just inside the resort's high cedar fences. He should take time for some stretches, he thought, watching absently as a small daysailer came into sight through the trees. The sail was scarlet against the blue water, luffing as the sole crew member smartly brought the boat around the end of the wharf.

It was a woman, her long blond hair blowing free in the breeze. She was wearing shorts and a brief top, white sneakers on her feet. With smooth expertise she docked the daysailer, throwing a line over the cleat on the wharf and tightening it before leaping ashore.

It couldn't be.

It was.

His mouth suddenly dry, Luke loped the last few yards toward the wharf. The woman had her back to him as she finished mooring the boat, her spine a long curve, her hair gleaming in the sun. Stepping onto the gently swaying wooden planks, he said, "Good morning, Katrin."

She gave an exaggerated start. Then she tied a couple of untidy half hitches, dropped the rest of the rope and stood up, turning to face him. She pushed her dark glasses up into her hair; her eyes, a glacial blue this morning, fastened themselves on his face. "What are you doing here?"

"You're a pro," he said easily. "You handled the boat beautifully—is it yours?"

"My question came first."

He swiped at his forehead with the back of one hand, and said with a winning smile, "I'm trying to work off last night's pork tenderloin. Not to mention the orange mousse.''

As though she couldn't help herself, her gaze skidded down his chest, its pelt of dark hair visible through his wet top, to the flatness of his belly. She took a sudden step back. Luke grabbed at her arm. "Watch it, you don't want to fall in.''

Her skin was warm from the sun. She shook her elbow free, patches of color in her cheeks. "I've got to go,'' she muttered. "I'll be late for work.''

His glance flickered down her body. Her breasts pushed against her thin green top, the faint shadow of her cleavage visible at the scooped neck; her legs were slim and lightly tanned. It wasn't an opportune moment to remember Guy's question... *you hiding anything else under that uniform?* Luke now knew what she'd been hiding. Trying to gather his wits, he repeated, "Do you own the boat?''

"Yes,'' she snapped, "I bought it with my investments.''

Ignoring this, Luke said tritely, "Nice lines.'' The same, of course, could apply to her. "Do you do much sailing?''

"Whenever I can.'' She lifted her chin. "It gets me away from the dining room. In more ways than one. Keeps my sanity, in other words.''

"There are a great many other jobs that would suit you better.''

"You're repeating yourself.''

"You're not getting it.''

"Life isn't quite as simple as you seem to think it is. Sir.''

If anyone knew life wasn't simple, it was himself. Holding tight to his temper, Luke said more moderately, "I'm sorry, I'm being tactless. I'd hate to see you stuck here year after year when there are wider horizons, that's all.''

"Fine. I get the message.''

"I'm also sorry about Guy," Luke went on. "He's a grade-A jerk who shouldn't go near a bottle of booze."

"I can look after types like him."

"So I noticed."

"The brandy was an accident."

"And the sail on your boat's purple."

For a brief moment laughter glinted in her eyes. He'd already decided she had beautiful eyes. Now add the rest of her, he thought. Although *beautiful* was a much overused word that didn't really encompass her grace, femininity and unconscious pride; the luster of her skin, the smooth flow of her muscles; the sexual pull she was exerting on him without—he was almost sure of this—in any way intending or wanting to.

But wasn't this all irrelevant? He met lots of beautiful women, so many that he should be immune to outward appearances by now; and the only reason his heart was thumping in his chest was that he'd been running for the better part of sixty minutes. Nothing to do with Katrin. He said abruptly, "I don't even know your full name."

"You don't need to."

Smiling broadly, Luke held out his hand. "Luke MacRae."

Katrin looked down at his hand, her own firmly at her sides. The wind blew a strand of hair across her face. "I already told you, staff and guests don't fraternize. I could get in real trouble if someone sees us talking like this."

"Then it's too bad there isn't a bottle of brandy close by."

Again wayward laughter briefly warmed her blue irises; and was as swiftly tamped. Her whole face changed when she laughed, becoming vibrant and full of mischief. Luke discovered that he very badly wanted to make her laugh again, although he had no idea how to go about it. He said, reaching for her right hand, "How's your cut, by the way?"

Her fingers lay tense in his palm. The bandage was still in place. He said flatly, "The mark is gone where Guy grabbed you."

This time there was no mistaking the emotion in her voice: it was panic. "Let go...I'll be late!"

"Why do I scare you?" Luke said slowly.

"I don't know. You don't! Why should you?"

He watched her swallow, the tendons moving in her throat where sunlight gilded skin like satin. He wanted to rest his fingers there. Feel the pulse in that little hollow race to his touch. Then let them drift across the delicate arch of her collarbone to the soft swell of her breast...he felt his own body tighten, every nerve on high alert.

He'd felt desire before. Many times. But never quite like this. So instinctual and imperative. So all-encompassing. He said with a deliberate lack of emphasis, "I think you're by far the loveliest woman I've ever seen."

If he'd expected Katrin to be flustered by his remark, or pleased, he was soon disappointed. She folded her arms across her chest, her eyes narrowing. "Do you?" she said. "Perhaps you're beginning to understand why I wear those awful glasses in the dining room—to discourage cheap compliments from men like you."

"Every word I said was the literal truth."

"And the sails on my boat are purple," she mocked.

"It's no crime to be beautiful, Katrin."

"Maybe not. But it's sure a liability in a job like mine. This conversation proves my point."

"You're stereotyping me!"

"Deny that you gave me the once-over a moment ago."

He couldn't. Trying to iron any emotion out of his voice, Luke said, "You're a very desirable woman. You know it, and so do I."

She hugged herself tighter. "I hate flattery."

Suddenly it was blindingly obvious to Luke. He said with

all the subtlety of a fourteen-year-old, "You want me just as much as I want you. That's why you're scared."

His words hung in the air; waves lapped the wharf, and overhead a gull wailed mournfully. Katrin whispered, "You're out of your mind."

He was. No question of that. "But I'm right. Aren't I?"

"No! You're the one who's after me—not the other way around. And it's because I'm just a waitress," she added with a depth of bitterness that shocked him. She snatched her hand free. "I'm yours for the asking. Cheap. Available. It's fine for you—you can jet in and jet out. But I'm stuck with—"

"This has nothing to do with how you earn your living," Luke said fiercely.

"Yeah, right." She pushed her hair back; in the sunlight, it gleamed like ripe prairie wheat. "You asked my name. It's Katrin Sigurdson. My husband's name is Erik Sigurdson. He's a fisherman. He's out there on the lake right now."

It was as though she'd punched Luke hard in the solar plexus. He rasped, "You don't wear a ring."

"My wedding band's antique gold, very finely engraved... I choose not to wear it at work. Or sailing."

Was she telling the truth? She was staring straight at him, conviction in every line of her body. Conviction, defiance, and something else: a trace of the panic he'd seen before? "Are you from here?" he asked, trying to gather his wits.

"Yes. I've lived here all my life."

"So I haven't seen you anywhere else..."

"Not unless you've been here before. How could you have?"

How indeed? Baffled, frustrated and at some deep level frightened in a way he wasn't about to admit to himself or her, Luke said bluntly, "Then I was wrong. You don't remind me of anyone. If you don't want to be late for work, you'd better go."

Her expression was guarded; certainly he could discern not the slightest trace of relief. She said, "One more thing. Leave me alone from now on. Strictly alone. That way maybe I'll believe you're not just another tourist on the make." Then she turned on her heel and walked away from him.

She moved with a lissome grace: something else her shapeless uniform had disguised. As she entered a grove of poplars, sunshine and shadow played in her hair, sprinkling the curves of her hips and slender lines of her thighs. Luke discovered his fists were clenched at his sides, his breathing trapped in his throat. What was wrong with him?

She was married. Unavailable.

Her ugly glasses and unflattering hairdo were to deflect unwanted male attention. She wasn't in disguise. There was no mystery after all.

Luke pulled first one heel then the other to his buttocks, stretching his quads. He never behaved like this around a woman. Pushing her for answers. Wanting to know everything about her. Pursuing her. For one thing, he never needed to: the women came to him. For another, his whole focus since he'd run away from Teal Lake at age fifteen had been work. Unrelenting work. Be it underground in mines in the north, then aboveground everywhere else. He'd spent years reading, making contacts, investing his carefully hoarded savings and traveling the world over. He'd endured late hours and setbacks. There'd been times when he thought he was going under, so close to it he could taste defeat, smell the sourness of failure. But he hadn't gone under. He'd made it to the top, to the sweet smell of success.

And all because he'd driven himself unmercifully. If his expectations for his staff were high, his expectations for himself were astronomical. Work was central to his life, its driving force. Women were peripheral. Decorative, pleasant, but definitely on the sidelines. And that's where he intended to keep them.

There'd been women during those years, of course. He was no monk. But they had to be the kind who'd accept his conditions. No commitment with nothing long-term.

Although there hadn't been nearly as many women as some of his colleagues might think.

And now, for no reason that he could discern, a mysterious, argumentative, independent blonde had gotten through all his defenses. A married woman, no less.

He never involved himself with anyone married. He abhorred infidelity. Besides, he thought meanly, his preference was for tall brunettes, and Katrin Sigurdson was of average height and blond into the bargain.

Would he ever forget the way the sun had threaded her hair with gold? Or the delicate shadows under her cheekbones? And then there was her body, so graceful, so exquisitely curved. Calling to him in a way that made nonsense of all his self-imposed rules and defenses.

Because defenses they were. His childhood and adolescence had killed something in him. The ability to love, to reach out to another human being and show his vulnerability. All the gentler emotions, like tenderness and protectiveness, had gone underground. He could add to the list, he thought savagely. But why bother? He was the way he was. And that was that.

He wasn't going to change now.

Not for anyone. And certainly not for a married woman who didn't even want to pass the time of day with him.

Luke thudded his foot back on the wharf, stretching his calf. Enough, he thought. More than enough. Right now he was going back to his room to shower, then he was heading for breakfast. And not once at breakfast or dinner was he going to make as much as eye contact with Katrin Sigurdson.

Luke made sure he walked into the dining room that morning accompanied by John, Akasaru and Rupert, who were engaged in an animated discussion about pollution control. Katrin was waiting on their table, wearing her plastic glasses. As if she weren't there, Luke sat down and ordered his standard breakfast. "And coffee," he finished with an edge of impatience. "Right away."

"Certainly, sir."

Certainly, sir. Luke gritted his teeth, and started discussing the effectiveness of the scrubbers a couple of refineries were using in Hamilton area. Gradually he became aware that Martin and Hans, across the table, were talking about a fishing expedition that had taken place that very morning, during which Martin had landed several pickerel. "We spoke to Katrin," Hans said in his heavy German accent. "The chef, he will cook them for us for supper. That is right, not so, Katrin?"

"That's right, sir. He does an excellent job with fresh fish."

"I'm planning to try the local goldeye this evening," John intervened. "I hear it's very tasty."

Olaf, the maître d', was just arriving with a new pot of coffee. Luke said in a carrying voice, "I gather Katrin's husband is a lake fisherman—perhaps we'll be sampling his catch this evening."

Olaf stopped in midstride, giving Katrin a puzzled look. She glared at him, her cheeks pink, took the sterling silver pot from him, and said dismissively, "Thanks, Olaf."

"Married, eh?" Guy said, as she reached over to refill his cup. "Lucky fellow...so when did you tie the knot, Katrin?"

Several drops of coffee spilled on the immaculate linen tablecloth. She said evenly, "I'm so sorry, sir...oh, it was quite a while ago."

"Like two years?" Guy persisted.

She flinched, her fingers curled tightly around the handle of the coffeepot. "Several years ago, sir."

"And you did say he was a fisherman, didn't you?" Luke asked with deliberate provocation, looking right at her even though he'd sworn he wasn't going to.

She held his gaze. "Yes, I did."

If she was lying, she was a pro. And if she wasn't, he had to give her full marks for poise. For a wild moment Luke played with the idea of jumping up, pulling the glasses from her face and kissing her with all his pent-up frustration. Would that tell him the truth about Katrin Sigurdson?

John said casually, "I hear the storms can be very dangerous on the lake."

"That's correct, sir. It's because the lake's so large and the water's shallow—consequently, big waves can arise very quickly. A south wind is particularly bad. But the fishermen know all the weather signals, and head for shore before they run into trouble."

Luke said nothing. He wasn't going to kiss her in full view of a roomful of his peers. Of course he wasn't. He wasn't going to kiss her anywhere. He gulped down his excellent Colombian coffee, thinking very fast. Katrin's husband had been news to Olaf, Luke would swear to that on a stack of Bibles. So had she produced an entirely fictional husband for Luke's benefit down on the wharf? And was she now continuing that lie at the breakfast table?

There were ways he could find out. Although asking Olaf wasn't one of them. A guest asking questions about the marital status of a waitress would be a sure way to get that waitress in trouble. No, he wouldn't ask Olaf. However, there was a two-hour break in the proceedings right after lunch. He'd planned to corner the delegates from Peru; but that could wait until this evening.

He had to know if she was telling the truth. Because if she wasn't, then it raised the very interesting question of why she'd bothered lying to him.

Why would Katrin invent a husband who didn't exist? Was she afraid of Luke? Or of herself?

Either way, he wanted the answer.

CHAPTER FOUR

AT TWO o'clock that afternoon Luke unlocked his rental car and got in, dropping his camera on the passenger seat. It was a perfect summer day, warm with a breeze from the lake, fluffy white clouds skudding across a sky as blue as Katrin's eyes. He had no real plan in mind, other than driving to the nearby village and looking around, asking questions of anyone he happened to meet. The village of Askja was small. Everyone must know everyone else.

Certainly he could find out if a fisherman called Erik Sigurdson existed; and whether he had a wife called Katrin.

He'd played with the idea of asking the desk clerk where Katrin lived, and had abandoned it because he couldn't think of a plausible reason why he should want such information. Whether she was married or not, he didn't want to cause her any problems at work. She must have her reasons for taking a job that didn't use her intelligence and caged her spirit; it wasn't up to him to upset that particular apple cart.

He left the grounds of the resort, taking the turnoff to the village. The road was narrow, following the lakeshore. Little whitecaps dotted the water like seabirds; a lighthouse, brightly striped in red and white, stood guard over a long, tree-clad promontory where gulls soared the air currents. It was a peaceful scene. But Luke had grown up at much the same latitude, and knew how long and brutal the winters could be; for the early Icelandic settlers, this must have been a cruel and unforgiving landscape.

He took a couple of photos of a weathered gray barn, of sheep munching the grass in a fenced field and a solitary cow chewing her cud. A small stone church stood watch over lichen-coated gravestones and neatly mowed grass; along the village wharf, fishing boats were rocking at their moorings, their white flanks gleaming. He didn't want to take a photo of the boats. What if he found out Katrin wasn't lying? That one of those boats belonged to her husband Erik? What then?

He'd turn around and go back to work. That's what he'd do. And he'd forget her existence in three days' time when the conference ended and he flew to New York for a series of meetings.

The houses were small, set apart in a long curve that followed the shoreline, most with a fenced garden. He'd drive the length of the village first, then he'd turn around and go into the general store. Or into that tearoom.

The last house was painted pale yellow, with a rhubarb patch, hills of potatoes, and neat rows of peas and beans. On the sand beach in front of the house, a woman and two children were playing with a Frisbee. Luke jammed on the brakes. He'd have known the woman anywhere, even though her hair was hidden under a baseball cap. She was wearing the same shorts and top that she'd had on this morning.

She hadn't said anything about children.

His heart beating in thick, heavy strokes, Luke looped the camera around his neck, got out of his car and walked through the trees toward the sand. He felt overdressed in his lightweight slacks and cotton shirt; he felt like a kid on his first date.

He stopped and, using his zoom lens, brought Katrin into focus, her legs a blur of movement, her teeth a dazzling white as she laughed. She was so intent on the game that she hadn't seen him yet. In quick succession he took three photos of her, hating her for being so carefree when he felt anything but.

As he lowered the camera, one of the children yelled something to her, and Katrin pivoted to face him. Her body went rigid. Then she tugged at the strap of her tank top and swiped at her forehead. ''Are you looking for someone?'' she called in a voice no one would have described as friendly.

Okay, Luke. Go for it.

He plastered a smile on his face, hung his camera over the branch of a small apple tree, and loped down to the beach. ''Hi, Katrin,'' he said. ''I had a couple of hours off, so I decided to check out the village...it's a gorgeous day, isn't it?'' Without waiting for a reply, he grinned at the nearest child, a girl of about seven with pale blond hair in two long pigtails. ''I'm staying at the resort. It's been a long time since I've played with a Frisbee...do you mind if I join you?''

She gave him a gap-toothed smile. ''You can be on my team,'' she said. ''What's your name?''

''Luke. What's yours?''

''Lara,'' she replied, and tossed him the plastic disc.

Lara Sigurdson? Daughter of Katrin? Discovering he wasn't ready for the answer to that question, Luke watched the Frisbee whirl toward him in a graceful arc. His muscles seemed to have seized up. Awkwardly he grabbed for it, then with a wicked twist of his wrist threw it toward Katrin. For a split second she stood stock still, glaring at him.

''Get it!'' the little boy shouted. He also was blond, about five, thin as whip.

The same age Luke had been when his mother had left.

Katrin leaped sideways, her arm upstretched, and caught the Frisbee. She tossed it to the boy. ''Run, Tomas!''

Tomas ran the wrong way, doubled back and clutched the Frisbee to his shirtfront. When he threw it toward Lara, it smacked into the sand. Lara said gleefully, ''Our point.''

She aimed it at Katrin, who then with the strength of

fury whipped it through the air straight at Luke's chest. He began to laugh, a helpless belly laugh, jumped to his right so it wouldn't break his ribs, and snagged it from midair. His shoes weren't intended for the beach; he skidded on the sand, saving himself at the last minute from falling to the ground. "Good shot," he said appreciatively, and sent the Frisbee to Tomas with just enough spin to be a challenge, but not so much that the little boy couldn't catch it. Tomas's hand closed around it; this time his throw was to Luke, a wildly off-course throw that somehow Luke managed to land.

He was enjoying himself, Luke realized, laughing at the little boy. How long since he'd done something like this?

Not since he'd played with his friend Ramon's children in the spring, back in San Francisco.

In quick succession Katrin scored two points on Luke, who then proceeded to gain them back; she was playing in deadly earnest, he could tell, and laughed at her openly as she missed an underhanded shot he'd flashed her way. Then Tomas snaked a shot at him that he hadn't been expecting; his eyes glued to the white disc, he ran for it, his hand outstretched. Lara shouted a warning. And Luke ran smack into Katrin.

The two of them tumbled to the soft sand in a tangle of arms and legs. Somehow Luke ended up with his cheek jammed into her chest, one leg under her, his other thigh flung over her hip. She was breathing rapidly, her breasts enticingly soft. She smelled delicious, a dizzying combination of sunshine and that same delicate floral scent he remembered from the dining room.

His body hardened. He shifted hastily, not wanting her to know how instantly and fiercely he wanted her; and felt, as he moved against her, the tightening of her nipples. With all his self-control he fought against the urge to take her in his arms and find her mouth with his. Kiss her so he could taste the sunshine on her skin, the heat of her flesh.

Footsteps padded across the sand toward them. "Are you guys okay?" Tomas huffed. "You look kind of funny—all tangled up like an octopus."

Swiftly Luke rolled over on his stomach, distancing himself from Katrin, who leaped to her feet and said breathlessly, "We're fine. That was a great shot, Tomas."

"It was our point," Tomas said complacently. "Whose turn is it now?"

Luke hauled himself to his feet, grabbed the Frisbee and flung it with very little finesse at Lara. He felt as though he'd been hit with a ton of bricks. He felt punch-drunk, wired and lustful.

Just as well the kids were here, he thought with a crazy edge of laughter. Or he'd have rolled Katrin onto her back on the sand, fallen on top of her and kissed her until neither one of them could breathe; until making love with each other was the only possible option. Then, out of the corner of his eye, he saw the Frisbee coming at him; catching it, he whipped it toward Tomas.

He didn't dare look at Katrin.

Five minutes later, the little boy plunked himself down on the sand. "Time out," he puffed. "I'm too hot."

"Me, too," Lara echoed.

Katrin smiled at them. "Why don't you both go up to the house and get yourselves ice-cream cones? You know where they are. Don't forget to shut the freezer afterward."

"Two scoops?" Lara said, her blue eyes calculating.

Katrin grinned. "Two scoops. But not three, you know what happened last time."

"Splat," said Tomas.

"Exactly," Katrin said. "Off you go, and look both ways before you cross the road. I'll be up in a minute."

The two children, forgetting they were tired and hot, ran

for the house, obediently stopping on the grass verge and checking for traffic. By the time they were out of earshot, Katrin had turned her back on them to face Luke. Her smile had vanished. "How dare you invade my private life?" she blazed. "You've got no right to be here, forcing yourself on my children like that."

A cold fist squeezed his heart. "So they're your children?"

"Who else's would they be?" she retorted. "I don't want you anywhere near here—I keep my work life and my personal life totally separate. Besides, I told you to leave me alone, remember?"

He said reluctantly, "They're fine kids."

"Yes, they are. And if you think I'm going to have some kind of a two-day fling with you and jeopardize my whole life, you're crazy."

Luke's tongue felt thick, and his brain seemed to have stopped working altogether. Katrin was married, the mother of two children. What the hell was he doing here? He swallowed, clearing his throat. "Let's keep something straight. I've not once suggested I wanted a fling with you."

She flushed, shoving her hands into the pockets of her shorts. "Don't insult my intelligence—I can read the signals."

"Then you're quite intelligent enough to know that some very basic chemistry's operating between us. It's not just me."

"It is just you!"

Her cheeks were now a bright pink. Luke drawled, "We could have one of those exchanges best suited to Tomas and Lara. It's not. It is. It's not. It is…is that what you want?"

"I want you gone from here. And I don't want you to come back," she said with deadly precision.

He had the same sinking feeling in his gut that had overcome him ten years ago when he'd been outwitted by a broker whose financial wizardry had been exceeded only by his lack of morals. Now, as then, there was no way to recoup. His only recourse was to get out as gracefully as he could and accept his losses. He said with a sudden raw honesty that took him by surprise, "Okay. I'll leave and I won't come back. But I won't find it easy to forget you...don't ask me to explain that, because I can't. And don't for one minute think I make a habit of hitting on women when I'm at a conference. Nothing could be further from the truth—and that holds whether they're waitresses or CEOs."

He'd run out of words. There was nothing else to say that could make any difference. Game over.

As though he were taking another photograph, Luke found himself trying to memorize every detail as Katrin stood before him: the elegant lines of her cheekbones, the sudden uncertainty in her sky-blue eyes, the push of her breasts against her thin green top. Storing it all in his brain against the time when he'd be gone from here. When he'd never see her again.

She said stiffly, "Give me one good reason why I should believe you."

"I can't! Either you believe me or you don't. And what does it matter anyway?"

"You're right, it doesn't matter." She bit her lip. "Please leave now, Luke—I should go up to the house and make sure the kids are all right. Besides, Erik will be home shortly."

The last person in the world Luke wanted to meet was Katrin's husband. The man who shared her bed. The father of her children. With one small part of his mind he realized that this was the first time Katrin had called him by name, and would also be the last. "Goodbye, Katrin," he said, turned on his heel and wound through the poplars toward his car, remembering on the way to snag his camera from the apple tree.

Just as he opened the car door, Lara and Tomas emerged onto the front step of the house, each clutching an ice-cream cone. They waved at him. "Bye, Luke," Lara called.

"Goodbye, Lara. Bye, Tomas," he called back, turned around in the road and drove north along the shore. In his rearview mirror he watched Katrin cross the road and walk toward the house.

Game over, indeed.

Except it didn't remotely resemble a game. Rather, Luke felt like that little five-year-old boy in Teal Lake who'd finally realized his mother wasn't going to come back home; that she hadn't just gone to the store, or into Kenora for a visit. Then, as now, he had the same sensation that the earth had shifted, that there was nothing firm to stand on.

Katrin was married, the mother of two children. No matter how much he desired her, she belonged to someone else.

Once Luke was out of sight of the pale yellow house, he pulled up by the side of the road and gazed out over the lake. Its serenity mocked him, so placid was it, so much in harmony with the graceful willows that draped its shoreline.

He felt cheated. As though he'd caught a glimpse of beauty beyond his imagining, only to have it snatched away before he could grasp it.

A couple of teenage boys were slouching along the road toward him. Luke edged off the shoulder and drove on. But five minutes later, when the tearoom came in sight, he slowed down again. He didn't want to go back to the resort and be convivial. He didn't want to play golf or lift weights, and he'd already jogged this morning. While tearooms weren't priority on his list, he could do with something cold to drink. And maybe a piece of chocolate pie, he thought wryly. The basic cure for a bruised ego.

Because that's all this was. It wasn't a major tragedy. He'd merely made a fool of himself for reasons he didn't want to analyze, with a woman far too acute for his own comfort. Yeah, he thought, turning into the driveway between rows of pink and scarlet petunias. Chocolate pie. That's what I need.

The tearoom wasn't designed with six-foot-two men in mind: the tables were small, the curtains frilly, the wallpaper with more flowers than a Hollywood funeral. But in the cooler by the door there was a chocolate torte with thick layers of dark chocolate icing, and the proprietress gave him a friendly welcome. Luke smiled back. "I'll have a big slice of the torte," he said, "and iced tea with extra lemon, please."

"Coming right up," she said, her brown eyes twinkling at him. Her name tag was inscribed in such elaborate calligraphy that he had difficulty deciphering it; he was almost sure it said Margret. Her hair was the orange of marigolds, her eyeshadow blue as delphiniums, and she had no pretensions to youth. But something in her smile said that a tall, athletic-looking man could brighten her day anytime.

Luke picked up a newspaper from the stand by the door and sat down by the window. Six women were sharing a table on the far side of the room, and two more were seated nearer to him; he was the only man. Feeling minimally more cheerful, he unfolded the paper. When his iced tea arrived, he took a sip; it was exactly as he liked it. Then Margret arrived with a flowered plate bearing a huge slab of torte surrounded by swirls of chocolate sauce, sliced strawberries and whipped cream. He grinned. "No calories in that."

"You're in fine shape, you don't need to worry," she said, giving him a flirtatious wink. "You must be staying at the resort?"

"That's right, there's a mining conference going on."

Deliberately he added, "I was just driving through the village and met Katrin, who's our waitress in the dining room."

"Katrin Sigurdson, that's right. She lives in the pink house two down from the church."

Luke's fork stopped in midair. "No...she was at the very end house in the village. Playing with her kids."

Margret frowned. "Kids?"

"Lara and Tomas. Blond like her."

"Katrin doesn't have any children." Margret's brow cleared. "Those are Anna's children." In a carrying voice she addressed one of the two women seated nearby. "Anna, is Katrin looking after your kids today?"

Anna, who had a cluster of blond curls and light blue eyes, smiled at Margret. "She offered to take them to the beach for an hour so Fjola and I could meet here and have an uninterrupted visit." Her smile encompassed Luke. "Katrin's such a lovely person. So kind. And the children adore her, they'd do anything for her."

Anna, he could tell, was the sort of woman who'd grown up in a small place and trusted everyone, including himself. Striving for just the right touch of lightness, he said, "Then it's to be hoped she has children of her own someday."

Anna chuckled. "First she has to find a husband."

Luke's heart jolted in his chest. "She's a pretty woman," he said with deliberate understatement. "That shouldn't be a problem."

"But Katrin is very choosy, too choosy for a little village like Askja." Anna shrugged. "She is talking of leaving here. That will be our loss, but no doubt her gain." She gave Luke another of her generous smiles. "Now, if you will excuse me..."

She went back to her conversation with her friend Fjola. Luke said, "Margret, I've heard that a fisherman called Erik Sigurdson takes tourists out in his boat, is that right?"

"Erik? Yes, but only on weekends. He's too old now to do it every day, he says." Her smile had a touch of malice. "Too fond of the rum bottle if you ask me."

"Too bad... I'll be gone by the weekend."

"Jonas takes out tourists every day, the resort would have his phone number."

"Thanks," Luke said. "I'll probably look him up."

Three more women came in the door and Margret left to show them to a table. Luke stared unseeingly at the newspaper. So Katrin was neither a married woman nor a mother.

She'd lied to him.

For her own protection? Because she was afraid of him, and put him in the same category as Guy? Or because he'd been reading her correctly all along, and Katrin wanted him as badly as he wanted her?

The latter couldn't be true. She'd been doing her level best to discourage him ever since they'd met.

His initial assessment of her as deadly dull had been way off the mark. So maybe when it came to her sexuality he was misreading her again.

Luke gazed at his torte, discovering that he'd entirely lost his appetite. However, he had the feeling Margret would take it personally if he didn't finish every morsel on his plate. He picked up his fork, his thoughts marching on. He now knew where Katrin lived and that she was thinking of leaving Askja.

He could invite her to San Francisco.

Sure, he jeered. You're really into rejection, Luke MacRae. She'd laugh in your face. And if by any chance she did agree, she'd turn your life upside down, you can be sure of that. Is that what you want?

No. Definitely not. His life was fine as it was.

The torte was moist with chocolate, the strawberries slightly tart. Luke began to eat, trying simultaneously to make some sense out of the latest financial predictions; but when he left the tearoom twenty minutes later, after a serious overdose of chocolate, he realized he was in a foul mood. Oh, he'd been all very clever the last couple of hours. Chief Detective MacRae in action, ferreting out the truth about the marital status of a waitress in a little fishing village in Manitoba. But what good did his new knowledge do him?

Katrin Sigurdson spelled danger. And what was a sensible tactic when face-to-face with danger? Avoid it. He wasn't a reckless eighteen-year-old anymore, he had no bent toward self-destruction; and he'd proved himself often enough in the past, he didn't need to do so again. Not with a blue-eyed blonde who could tear apart everything he'd so carefully constructed.

Stay away from her. That was all he needed to do.

It was so simple.

CHAPTER FIVE

FOR twenty-four hours Luke did stay away from Katrin. He got back to the lodge that afternoon late for a panel discussion, which did nothing to improve his state of mind. He then set up a private consultation with the Peruvian delegates in his suite, ordering room service for dinner. Afterward, he worked far into the night, fell into an exhausted sleep, and was also late for breakfast because he'd forgotten to set his alarm.

At least he hadn't dreamed about her. He'd been spared that.

When he took his seat in the dining room, he soon discovered it was Katrin's day off; a young man called Stan waited on them. Again Luke drove himself hard all day. But by four-thirty he'd done everything that needed to be done, and he was in no mood to drift to the bar and exchange small talk. He decided to go for a run instead.

He jogged for the better part of an hour, watching distant purple-edged clouds move closer and closer, until they merged into a dark mass that spread all the way to the horizon. When he passed the wharf below the resort, he noticed with an edge of unease that the daysailer was gone from its mooring.

The wind had come up in the last few minutes. A south wind, he realized, his unease growing. Hadn't Katrin said that was the most dangerous wind on the lake?

It was her day off. Wasn't it all too likely that she'd gone sailing?

What had she said? It kept her sanity?

When he needed a break from the pressures of work, he jogged, played tennis and skied. It was the same principle.

A sudden gust whipped through his hair. Fear lending wings to his feet, Luke ran back to the lodge, changed in his room into jeans and a T-shirt, and raced for his car. First he checked the resort wharf again, but there was still no daysailer. Then he drove fast to the village wharf. Again, no slim white boat with a furled scarlet sail. By now, waves were lashing the wharf, the spray driven against the thick boards.

An old man was climbing the metal ladder from his boat to the dock. Luke strode over to him, raising his voice over the gusts of wind. "I'm looking for Katrin Sigurdson—she uses a small boat with a red sail. Do you know if she's out on the lake?"

The old man had red-veined cheeks and bleary blue eyes. "Katrin? That's my niece…I'm Erik Sigurdson."

"Luke MacRae," Luke said, shaking hands. How it must have amused Katrin to posit her disreputable uncle as her husband. He repeated urgently, "I'm worried about her, surely she wouldn't stay out in weather like this?"

"Katrin?" The old man gave an uncouth cackle. "Too smart for that. Although she likes pushing herself, I must say. I've said to her more than once, you'll go too far one day, my girl, and then what'll—"

"Then where is she?"

"You're in a right state, young feller," Erik said, spitting with careless accuracy into the churning water.

Luke said tightly, "Yes, I am. So why don't you answer the question?"

"She ain't interested in guys from the resort. Here today and gone tomorrow, that's what she says."

Each word dropping like a chip of ice, Luke said, "I may be staying at the resort, but even I can tell there's a storm brewing on the lake. No one, but no one, should be out there in this kind of wind, especially in a skimpy little daysailer. So will you for God's sake tell me if you know where she is?''

''If she's not home and the boat's gone, she likely docked on the far side of the island. In the lee.''

''How do I get there?''

Erik took a square of tobacco from one pocket of his flannel shirt, a jackknife from the other, and with its viciously sharp blade cut off a chunk of tobacco. ''You got designs on my niece, Mr. Luke MacRae?''

''No. But I sure don't want her drowning while you and I stand here passing the time of day!''

''Okay, okay, no need to get antsy. Get in your car, turn right, take the next left and keep going to the end of the road. And I'll bet my entire supply of 'baccy that she's there.''

''I hope you're right,'' Luke snarled, and ran for his car. In a screech of tires he turned right. The first drop of rain plopped on his windshield. The limbs of the birches were tossing in the wind; clouds skudded across the lurid sky. Then he was suddenly enveloped in a downpour as a flash of lightning split the horizon in two.

Strong winds and lightning were deadly enemies of sailors. Fear knotting his muscles, Luke drove as fast as he dared through the rain and the gathering gloom. He should have asked how far before he turned left, he thought, furious with himself for the oversight. But he'd been so desperate to get away from Erik Sigurdson, he'd overlooked that all-important question.

She had to be at the dock. She had to be.

He shoved his foot on the brake, then backed up ten feet. He'd almost missed the turnoff, a narrow road flanked by spruce and poplar, rain pelting its gravel surface and running in rivulets into the ditches. He turned onto the road beneath shadowed trees. Slowing down, flicking the wipers to high speed, Luke drove on. Rocks rattled under his wheels.

As suddenly as it had begun, the road opened into a clearing, then snaked down a short, steep hill toward the water. Almost miraculously, the wind had dropped: the broad bay that he'd glimpsed from the top of the hill was in the lee. Lightning ripped the sky apart, followed by a clap of thunder that made him wince. He took the slope as fast as he dared, then parked beside a tangle of boat cradles and overgrown shrubbery. His was the only car in sight.

Thrusting his door open, Luke got out. Earth and rocks had been heaped to make an artificial barrier from the lake, barring his view. He ran down the last of the slope, rounded the corner and saw in front of him a dark stretch of water, pebbled with raindrops, and a small wooden jetty.

A daysailer was moored at the jetty. Katrin was kneeling on the wet boards, searching for something in her duffel bag. Her back was toward him.

She was safe.

For a moment Luke stood still, all his pent-up breath whooshing from his lungs. She wasn't out on the lake. She hadn't drowned. She was right here in front of him. Safe.

She was also quite alone, and without any visible means of transportation.

Slowly he walked toward her, his hair already plastered to his skull, his T-shirt clinging to his chest. Another spectacular jag of lightning lit up the whole scene; her shirt was pink, her cap a fluorescent green. Like a drumroll, thunder ushered him onto the wharf.

Enter the hero, Luke thought. Although Katrin would more likely categorize him as the villain; and she had clearly no need of rescue, which is what heroes were supposed to do. As he stepped across the first couple of planks, the vibrations of his steps must have alerted her. She lifted her head sharply, gazing right at him; for a moment he saw

the exhilaration still on her face, her wide smile and dancing eyes.

The terror that had kept his foot hard on the accelerator
all the way across the island fled, replaced by a tumultuous
rage. He grated, "Why are you looking so damned pleased
with yourself?"

The laughter vanished from her face. She pushed herself
upright, swinging her bag in one hand. "If you really want
to know," she said coldly, "I was congratulating myself
on how well I handled the boat once the wind came up."

"You were a fool to be out in this weather!"

"Thank you for that resounding vote of confidence."

He stepped closer, water gurgling beneath the boards.
"A south wind and a lightning storm—are you crazy? Or
just plain suicidal?"

"Neither one," she flared. "Why don't you go back to
the resort where you belong, Luke MacRae? Where, in the-
ory at least, you know what you're talking about."

He took her by the arm, rain sluicing his face. "It so
happens that right now I do know what I'm talking about—
if you'd gotten in trouble out there, someone would have
had to rescue you. You'd have been risking the lives of
other people just so you could get some cheap thrills. I used
the wrong word—that's not crazy. It's totally irresponsi-
ble."

She tried to pull free, her blue eyes blazing. "You seem
to be forgetting something—I got back ahead of the storm
and I didn't risk anyone's life. Including my own. Anyway,
what the *hell* are you doing here? I can't tell you how much
I dislike you following me around like this."

Luke's answer was to grab her by the shoulders, pull her
toward him and kiss her hard on the mouth.

Her response was instant and unmistakable. She flung
her arms around his waist and kissed him back.
Passionately. Generously. Recklessly.

As the contact ripped through him, another stroke of lightning lit the wharf with an eerie blue light. Thunder rattled through the trees, where the wind moaned like a creature in distress. But Luke scarcely noticed.

Katrin was soaked to the skin; he circled her waist, drawing her closer, trying to shelter her. One hand moved up her spine until her long ponytail hung like wet rope over his forearm. Then her lips opened to the urgent probing of his tongue. She pressed herself against him, her fingertips digging into his back, kneading his muscles. In a dizzying surge of pure lust, Luke felt her tongue dance with his.

She wanted him just as much as he wanted her. He'd been right all along. Fiercely and wondrously grateful, he grasped her by the hips and pulled them toward him, so that she could be in no doubt of his response. The wet fabric of her jeans was clammy and cold beneath his palms; yet inwardly Luke was on fire.

She was moving against him with a kind of coltish awkwardness that was eager, yet somehow untutored. She couldn't be a virgin, he thought distantly. Of course not. Anna had said Katrin was choosy…but surely not to that extent? He muttered against her mouth, "Let's run for the car—you're soaked."

"So are you," she whispered, cupping his face in her palms, her eyes brilliant as stars, as eerily blue as the lightning.

She'd bewitched him, he thought. She could have been a spirit from the depths of the lake; yet simultaneously she was flesh and blood, wholly and utterly desirable.

With a muffled groan Luke kissed her again, moving his lips over hers in a voyage of discovery that he wanted never to end. Her cheekbones, the sweep of her forehead, the firm line of her jaw…he wanted to know them all, to put his mark on them so that they were his alone. "You're so beautiful,'' he whispered hoarsely, ''so incredibly responsive...you taste of raindrops.''

She gave him another of those passionate kisses, her fingers running through his wet hair and down his nape. She couldn't have missed his shudder of response. Again he felt the thrust of her hips against his groin. Overwhelmed by a hunger as primitive as the thunder that was shaking the sky, Luke said, ''Let's go to the car.''

Katrin suddenly pulled her head back, her breasts rising and falling against the hard wall of his chest; as the rattle of thunder died away, he watched her struggle back to a different reality. ''My bag,'' she muttered, ''I've got dry clothes in it.''

''Then we'll take it,'' Luke said, grinning at her with something of her own recklessness. ''Although I like that shirt just the way it is.''

She glanced down. Her nipples were tight, the thin cotton outlining them as though she were naked. She bit her lip. ''Luke, I—''

He leaned down, grabbed her bag, put his arms around her and lifted her from the ground. Luxuriating in her weight, he growled, ''Enough talk,'' and kissed her again, his blood thrumming through his veins.

''I can feel your heartbeat,'' she said, twisting in his arms as she rested her hand against his chest, her face rapt.

Had he ever wanted a woman the way he wanted Katrin? It was as though that first kiss had opened floodgates too long closed, loosing a torrent of desire Luke was helpless to resist. He took the slope in long strides, the runoff saturating his sneakers, rain lashing his face. With his chin he tried to tuck Katrin's head into his chest, craving to protect her; a far part of his brain noted that protectiveness. Noticed also that it was new to him. Completely new. Inexplicable. But very much there.

He shoved his thoughts away. This wasn't the time for

analysis. Reaching the car, he fumbled with the passenger door, and eased her onto the seat. Then he hurried around to his side, searching for the keys in his wet pocket. He'd get some heat in the car first.

He got in and slammed his door. In the sudden silence, shielded from the onslaught of the storm, Luke looked at the woman in the seat beside him.

In the few moments it had taken him to walk from one side of the car to the other, Katrin had retreated from him. Her bag was on her lap; she was hugging it to her chest as though to ward him off, her eyes wideheld in the gloom. At a loss, for this wasn't what he'd expected, Luke said with a lightness that didn't quite succeed, "It's okay—I don't bite."

"I must have been mad," she cried. "It was the storm, and fighting the waves on the lake, and then getting into the bay and knowing I'd made it—"

"Katrin," he said evenly, "we want each other. There's nothing wrong with that."

"There's everything wrong with it!"

"Look, before we get into a big discussion, I think you should get out of those wet clothes. Right now."

She gave him a hunted look. "Oh, no—I'm fine."

"I'll close my eyes," he said, exasperated. "Or I'll wait outside the car with my back to you. For Pete's sake, what do you think I am?"

"I don't know what you are. Who you are. How could I?"

"You don't trust me."

With an intensity that entranced him, she said, "I don't trust myself! Surely that must be as obvious to you as it is to me."

Laughter welled in his chest. He fought it down; Katrin would not, right now, appreciate being laughed at. He turned on the ignition and the fan, to get some heat in the car, and said deliberately, "Is that why you lied to me? About your husband, Erik, and your two lovely children, Lara and Tomas, blond-haired and blue-eyed just like you? Because I have something to tell you—in Margret's tearoom, your friend Anna informed me the children were hers...and then I met your uncle Erik on the wharf when I was looking for you half an hour ago. His shirt needing washing, his boots belonged in the garbage, and he was about to chew on a large lump of tobacco, no doubt using the lake as a spittoon. I must say I'm very glad he's not your husband."

Katrin glowered at him, if anything clutching her bag even tighter. "I had to tell you something! You think I was about to admit to you that ever since that first evening in the dining room I've been dreaming about you every night? X-rated dreams. Not the kind I could tell Lara or Tomas."

His jaw dropped. *"What?"*

"You heard what I said. I'm not going to repeat it."

Dazedly Luke said, "Is honesty your middle name?"

"Stupidity, more like."

She looked as edgy as a wild creature, as though she'd bolt if he made the slightest wrong move. "That kind of honesty's rare," Luke said.

Her grimace was endearing. "I never usually tell lies...it goes against the grain, so I'm very bad at it. I was amazed when you fell for all that stuff about my husband and my two kids. I figured you'd see through it right away."

"Maybe I'm the stupid one," Luke said dryly. "How about making me a promise? No more lies."

"Promises are made between people who mean something to each other."

He looked her straight in the eye. "This particular promise has to do with your own integrity."

She was the first to look away. "Okay," she said grudgingly.

"Good," said Luke. "Change your clothes, I'll be back in five minutes."

He got out of the car. The storm was moving off as fast as it had arrived, the lightning had abated, and even the rain had let up. He scrambled down the slope and sat down on some old boards, reflecting on what had happened.

He'd lost control down there on the wharf, when Katrin had so unexpectedly and wholeheartedly kissed him back. Lost it instantly and completely and uncharacteristically. He never lost control. No matter who the woman was or how long he'd been without one. Oh, physically he could let go, that wasn't the issue. But he always kept his emotions under wrap.

Not with Katrin. In the space of five minutes he'd felt passionately grateful, hugely protective, and fiercely possessive. Grateful? Because a woman had kissed him? Protective of a woman entirely capable of looking after herself? As for possessive, he neither wanted to possess another human being nor to be possessed by one. If honesty were Katrin's middle name, independence was his. He'd come to that conclusion at fifteen, and had seen no reason to change it since.

It was a good thing she'd been too shy or too frightened to change her clothes in front of him. He'd needed to get away from her. To take time out, to think with his brain cells instead of his hormones.

Danger. That was what Katrin spelled. He already knew that.

Danger or not, he still wanted her. More than he'd wanted anything or anyone for a very long time.

As a stray gust rustled through the shrubs behind him, a shower of raindrops trickled down his neck. Luke swiped them off, thinking furiously. If he really wanted Katrin, why couldn't he have her? On his terms?

She hadn't needed any persuading on the wharf.

He could persuade her again. Of course he could. Although he'd have to tell her what his terms were; it wouldn't be fair to deceive her on that score.

But if she accepted them, he could take her to bed.

How else was he going to get rid of this obsession with Katrin Sigurdson?

CHAPTER SIX

A LAST flicker of lightning lit the sky. Far across the lake thunder growled in a halfhearted way. Luke's thoughts marched on. Once he'd gone to bed with Katrin, he'd be leaving here. Flying to New York, then back home to San Francisco. He'd forget her.

Easy.

Was the five minutes up? He hoped so. It was cold sitting here, his shirt clinging to his back. Luke got to his feet and walked up the hill. Katrin was sitting bolt upright in the front seat, a pale yellow sweater swathing her body. Luke got in the car.

The sudden blast of heat made him shiver involuntarily. In quick distress, she said, "You're cold. Here, I've got an extra sweater."

"I'm fine," he said roughly. "Quit feeling sorry for me."

"I wasn't aware that I was."

"I don't need mothering!"

The words had come from nowhere, and instantly Luke wished them unsaid. Katrin said in an unfriendly voice, "If I felt the slightest bit motherly toward you, I wouldn't be having X-rated dreams."

"So tell me about them," he said.

"Are you kidding? Luke, take me home. Then you should go back to the resort and have a hot shower."

"I could have one at your place."

"Look, I know I—"

"Katrin," he said softly, "come here."

"No! We can't—" Then she gave a strangled yelp, for

Luke had leaned over and, with exquisite gentleness, pressed his mouth to hers. Her lips were soft and yielding, warmer than his. His head began to swim.

She shifted in her seat, nibbling very gently at his lower lip, her hands drifting down his throat to his shoulders. In every nerve in his body he was aware of these small movements, of her quickened breathing and the pliancy of her body as she, in turn, leaned toward him. Control, Luke thought. Control. Technique, not emotion. And deepened his kiss, easing closer to her. Then he let one hand move from her shoulder to the swell of her breast, tracing its fullness, feeling the shock ripple through her slender frame. He cupped her breast in his hand, his groin hardening imperiously.

"Katrin," he whispered, "I want you so much."

She was trembling very lightly. "I want you, too," she whispered. "But I don't do this, Luke...I never have affairs with the guests. It's nothing to do with the resort, it's one of my own rules."

"You think I don't know that?" Trying to banish the strain from her face, he added, "Those glasses you insist on wearing, and your hair pulled back tight as a halyard in a hurricane...they're not exactly a come-on."

She smiled weakly. "Self-defense."

"Very effective," he replied; and knew now was the time to be as truthful to her as she'd been with him. Feeling as though he were tossing dice with no idea how they'd fall, Luke said, "I should make something clear to you—I'm not into any kind of commitment. If we make love tonight, that would be that. I fly to New York the day after tomorrow, and I won't be back."

She said in a strange voice, "That's okay...I wouldn't want commitment. It's not a word in my vocabulary, either."

"Why not?" he flashed.

She stared down at the fingers, intertwined in her lap. "To be blunt, Luke, if we go to bed together it'll have nothing to do with making love. I want you out of my system—I'm sorry if that sounds crude, but that's the way it is. For some reason you get past every one of my defenses. I can't explain that, and I'm not going to try. But I need to get on with my life…and I don't need a man in it. It's time I left Askja. Past time, and for reasons that are nothing to do with you. So if you have conditions, so do I—no confidences and no questions. And no—to use your word—commitment."

Luke sat back in his seat. He didn't like having his own words thrown back at him. Didn't like it all. Because he wasn't used to it? Was it that simple?

A couple of women in the past had taken his usual spiel about commitment as a challenge, figuring they could change his mind. Katrin, obviously, wouldn't be like that. Katrin didn't want commitment any more than he did.

Nevertheless, didn't her stance suit his purposes admirably? He could make love with her and leave.

She'd be out of his system, too.

Precisely what he wanted.

He said flatly, "I accept." Quickly he put the car in gear, turned around in the clearing and drove up the hill toward the woods.

The road needed all his attention because the heavy rain had turned some sections to a glutinous mud, and dug deep channels into the ditches. Keeping his eyes straight ahead, Luke said, "At least tell me how old you are."

"Twenty-seven. And you?"

"Six years older. Were you born here?"

"I said no questions, Luke."

"Secrets in your past?" he said lazily.

"Of course not!"

All his senses on high alert, he heard the tension in her

voice, noticed the tightening of her hands in her lap, her sudden wariness. So she did have secrets. He said without inflection, "I have secrets, too. Don't we all?"

"I wouldn't know."

End of that conversation, thought Luke, and found he was intensely curious to know what secrets in Katrin's past would prevent her from even telling him where she was born. None of your business, he told himself; then found himself wondering if it could have anything to do with that elusive sense of recognition he'd had for a while, as though somewhere he'd seen her before. He said out loud, "Good, there's the main road."

Katrin said nothing. He flicked a glance at her. She was staring out the window at the wet trees and gleaming pavement, just as though he didn't exist. He felt a quiver of pure rage, and forced it down. What was he complaining about? Once again he'd found a woman who was willing to warm his bed—or in this case, her bed—on his terms. Nothing wrong with that, and everything right.

He drove on, in a silence that seemed to thicken with every minute. After he passed the lane to the resort, he had to navigate all the turns and twists of the road to the village. The church loomed out of the dusk, followed by a weathered clapboard house and then a small bungalow painted pale pink with white trim. Luke turned in the driveway and parked level with the back door.

"Let's go in," he said, striving to sound matter-of-fact. "If you've got a drier, maybe I could put my jeans and shirt in it for a few minutes."

"Luke, I can't do this," Katrin said in a strangled voice.

"It's perfectly normal to be nervous, Katrin. I'll use protection, and I'll be as good to you as I can be, I promise you that."

"Protection?" she snapped, glaring at him. "You mean you walk around with it all the time?"

He said, an ugly note in his voice, "I've already told you I'm not in the habit of picking up women at conferences...and I have a clean bill of health. But the last thing I ever want to do is start an unwanted child. There are enough of those already in the world."

"Were you one?" she said.

"Lay off!"

"I hit a nerve there, didn't I?" She gazed at him thoughtfully. "You mean you never want to have children?"

"You said no questions and no confidences. That works both ways."

"Okay, okay. But whether or not we've got protection is beside the point." She looked right at him. "I've changed my mind. I'm sorry, but I can't go to bed with you—no matter what kind of dreams I've been having."

A cold lump had settled in the pit of Luke's stomach. He said nastily, "Do you do this often—lead a guy on, then say no at the last minute?"

"No! I never do!"

"You could have fooled me."

"Are you one of those men who think a woman isn't allowed to say no?"

"Katrin, I know you want me and you know I want you. So what's the big deal if we go to bed together? We're not talking marriage and three kids."

"No," she said, her voice unreadable, "we're talking a one-night stand."

"That's right. Which suits both of us just fine."

"Down on the wharf, and then in the car, I thought it would suit me. So that I'd get you out of my system, isn't that what I said? But now I've realized the absolute last thing I need is a one-night stand. With you or anyone else. I've never gone to bed with anyone casually, as if sex were in the same league as a game of Frisbee or an afternoon sail on the lake. And I'm not going to start now."

Luke looked over at her. Her lower lip was set mutinously, her wet ponytail was trailing down her neck, and her bulky sweater almost completely hid the fact that she had breasts. She was as different from his usual women as a woman could be, he thought with uncomfortable honesty. No makeup, no fancy hairdo, no designer clothes. No sophistication. Quite possibly, very little experience. Because if there was one thing he'd stake his fortune on, it was that Katrin Sigurdson was speaking the truth.

She didn't deal in fancy footwork. In coyness or manipulation. Just the truth, no matter whether he wanted to hear it or not. Keeping her promise that she wouldn't lie to him again.

He said harshly, "I'm not sure casual is the right word for what happens when we kiss each other. For me, it's like the combination of an earthquake and a volcanic eruption...you wouldn't exactly call those casual." Then he gave an exasperated sigh. "I had no intention of saying that—the truth must be catching. Like the flu."

She said with suppressed violence, "I've never in my life kissed anyone the way I kissed you."

Luke looked at her in silence, emotion clogging his throat. Once again, Katrin was telling the truth. And once again, just by being herself, she'd knocked him sideways. Warning bells rang in his brain. If he was half as smart as he thought he was, he'd push her out of the car and drive hell-bent for leather in the opposite direction.

Any other woman he'd had an affair with had treated bed as just another playground. Like a game of tennis with no clothes on. But Katrin wasn't like that.

"Katrin," he said with sudden intensity, "why don't we go for it? Is life about running away from risk, taking the safe route time and again until finally you're buried under the ground and there aren't any more risks to take? Is that all there is to it?"

She said bitterly, "I took a big risk once, with a slick businessman like you. It backfired and I paid for my mistake. Paid and paid and paid. The answer's no, Luke. No."

"Who was he?"

"That's irrelevant."

Luke made one more try. "Listen, I'm going back to San Francisco—"

"Where?"

The color had drained from her cheeks; she looked suddenly older. Older, and horribly frightened. "What's the matter?" he demanded.

"You said you lived in New York!"

"I said I was flying to New York from here—I've got a couple of meetings there early in the week. But once they're over, I'll be heading home. Which is San Francisco. What's the big deal about that?"

Her struggle for control was painful to watch. Her knuckles bone-white with strain, she said tonelessly, "Luke, I'm exhausted, I've got to go in. I'm sorry if you thought I was leading you on, truly I wasn't. What happened on the wharf was more than I could have imagined…it did away with all my common sense and my rules. But I've had time to think now, and I know I'd regret it if we went to bed together. I have rules for a very good reason, and they've always stood me in good stead."

He wanted to know that reason, and knew better than to ask. His gaze trained on her face, he said softly, "If I kissed you again, you'd change your mind."

Her jaw tensed. "Please don't!"

"You don't have to worry—I've never once forced myself on a woman, and I'm not going to start with you."

"Anyway," she said with a flash of spirit, "can you imagine how I'd feel tomorrow morning when I'd have to take your order for breakfast? *Cream and sugar with your coffee, sir?* No way!" She leaned down and picked up her bag from the floor of the car. "Thank you for the drive," she added in a muffled voice. "Good night."

He could have stopped her. Very easily. Luke sat still, watching as she ran for the side door of the little bungalow, took a key out of her pocket and turned it in the lock. Then she slipped inside the house. A moment later he saw the dim glow of light through the chinks in the blinds.

He put the car in reverse and backed onto the road. Which did he need more, a hot shower because every garment he had on was wet, chilling him to the bone? Or a cold shower, to take his mind off sex? Sex with Katrin.

That's all it would have been, he thought furiously. Sex. Nothing less and nothing more.

How long since a woman had turned him down?

Too long, obviously.

The sun was setting behind the last of the storm clouds in a stunning display of orange, magenta and purple. He scowled at it, wishing he could fly home tomorrow. Or tonight. One thing was certain. He didn't care if he ever saw Katrin Sigurdson again.

Because he was a stubborn man who rarely allowed himself to acknowledge a setback, Luke went to breakfast early the next morning. The morning paper was folded under his arm. He was the first one at his table. He started reading the front page, and when an all-too-familiar voice said, "Coffee, sir?" he didn't even look up.

"Black, please," he said, and ostentatiously rustled the pages.

His coffee was poured without a drop being spilled. He added, "A large orange juice, waffles with strawberries and an order of bacon, no toast. Thanks."

"You're welcome," Katrin said in a voice that implied the opposite.

He forced himself to continue reading the latest story of

political patronage, not even looking up when she'd left the table. Rupert arrived, then John, and slowly Luke relaxed. When she brought his waffles, he saw in one glance that she looked as different from the passionate woman on the wharf as she could; her ugly glasses were firmly in place and her hair scraped back ruthlessly. Good, thought Luke. He didn't want any reminders of those shattering kisses in the rain.

He'd dreamed about her last night. Explicitly and at considerable length.

The sooner he left here, the better.

The day dragged on. Luke had both contributed to and gained from the conference; but now he couldn't wait for it to be over. Dinner was a full-fledged banquet and seemed to last forever. Guy drank far too much and in a distant way Luke was amused to see that the whole table was united in making it clear that Guy had better behave himself. As for Katrin, she was efficient and polite and a thousand miles away.

Which is where he'd be tomorrow.

The meal wound down, Luke was called on to add to the impromptu speeches, and people began drifting toward the bar. Guy, however, was taking his time. As though he were waiting for everyone else to leave, Luke thought uneasily, and moved over to have one last chat with the Japanese delegation. Then he went back to the table and said with a friendliness he was far from feeling, "Come on, Guy, I'll buy you a drink."

"I could tell you something," Guy mumbled.

"Oh?" Luke said casually. "What's that?"

Guy shot him a crafty look. "I'm going to tell her first," he said, swaying on his feet.

"Her?"

"Our esh-esteemed waitress."

"What about her?"

"Nope. Her first."

Under cover of the hum of conversation and laughter, Luke said very quietly, "You leave Katrin alone, Guy. Remember what I said about Amco Steel?"

"Thish-this is for her own good," Guy said, blinking owlishly.

"Then tell me about it."

"Tomorrow. At breakfast." Guy chuckled. "You'll have to wait, Luke."

"Fine," Luke said, as though it were of no interest to him whatsoever. "Let's go to the bar, that's where the action is right now."

For well over an hour, Luke wandered from group to group in the bar, never staying long, always trying to keep Guy in sight. But Andreas and Niko from Greece wanted to show him a fax they'd just received and when Luke looked up, Guy had vanished. He said, "Andreas, that's good news. I think we should have a talk about this once I get back to San Francisco, can I call you? And now will you excuse me, I want to talk to Guy Wharton for a moment."

When he questioned one of the waiters, the young man said he'd seen Guy heading for the side door of the resort. As Luke hurried along the corridor, he was stopped by an elderly statesman from Japan, who with impeccable courtesy wished him a protracted goodbye. Holding his impatience rigidly in check, Luke replied with equal good manners. Then, almost running, he headed outdoors.

The side door opened onto a walkway that split into two, one to the guest parking lot, the other to the staff lot. Trusting his intuition, Luke took the path to the staff area. To muffle his steps he kept on the grass, simultaneously wondering if he was overreacting. Was he really going to find Guy and Katrin together? He did know one thing: he didn't trust Guy, sober or drunk. Especially not drunk.

Then he stopped in his tracks as he heard voices, Guy's slurred, Katrin's quiet, but edged with panic. So they were together. Although not, by the sound of it, from Katrin's choice.

He was going to do his level best to protect her from whatever threat Guy posed.

But first he hoped to find out exactly what that threat was.

CHAPTER SEVEN

LUKE skirted the dogwood and tall shrub roses, whose scent teased his nostrils, and saw that Guy had cornered Katrin several feet away from the staff parking lot. Her back was to a clump of birch; Guy was looming over her, one hand clamped around her elbow. Although his stance was far from steady, he was talking with relative coherence.

"I e-mailed a friend of mine this afternoon," he was saying. "Wanted to be sure of the facts before I said anything. It was a friend in San Francisco."

Katrin flinched as though he'd physically struck her; with desperate strength she tried to tug her arm free. "I don't want to hear this," she said, "it's got nothing to do with me."

"Oh, yes, it does. We both know what I'm talking about." He gave an uncouth burst of laughter. "A stain on your reputation. How's that for starters?"

To Luke's puzzlement, Katrin suddenly sagged against the white trunk of one of the birches. She looked defeated, he thought. Broken. What the hell was going on?

Guy laughed again. "I see you understand what I'm talking about. Well, I've got a little proposition for you. You come to my room, say in ten minutes, and we'll forget the whole thing. But if you don't, I'll make sure before I leave here tomorrow morning that you don't have a job—they wouldn't want someone with your little secret working for them, now would they?"

Katrin said nothing. It wasn't just defeat, Luke thought. It was despair. As though Guy had pushed her too far, to a place where she was defenseless. What was her secret?

And why did she react like a startled deer whenever San Francisco was mentioned?

As though her silence infuriated him, Guy said nastily, "Room 334. In ten minutes—you be there, okay? If not, I'll smear your name over every newspaper in Manitoba and you won't get a job anywhere."

He dropped her elbow and started weaving along the path toward the lodge. Luke sank back into the shadowed bushes, thorns scratching his neck and hands. Then he stayed very still, scarcely breathing. Guy stumbled past, never once glancing at the rosebushes. When he'd vanished around a bend in the path, Luke carefully extricated himself from the branches. His suit would never be the same again, he thought, and in a few long strides reached the woman who was still cowering under the birch trees.

"Katrin," he said, "are you all right?"

She stared at him as though she'd never seen him before, as though he were some kind of apparition. She was trembling all over, Luke saw with a surge of compassion that rocked him to the roots. "What's wrong?" he said gently, and reached out for her.

She shrank from him. "Don't touch me," she quavered, "I can't stand it! Just go away. *Please.*"

"I can't do that…you're in some kind of trouble, aren't you? Tell me about it, and perhaps I can help."

Help? he thought blankly. Get involved? Him? Normally he never got involved in the lives of others.

"No one can help," Katrin said with such a depth of hopelessness in her voice that Luke was chilled to the bone.

"What was Guy talking about? What's this secret all about?"

Her shoulders drooped. "So you heard him."

"He let it drop after dinner that he had something to say to you. He's a bad actor, we both know that. Hell, the whole conference knows it. So I followed him here."

With none of her usual grace, Katrin pushed herself away from the tree. "Luke, this has nothing to do with you. Stay out of my life... I keep asking you, and you just don't get it."

"Are you going to his room?"

"So that's what's bothering you," she flared. "If you can't have me, then no one else can?"

Luke winced. Then he said in a hard voice, "Guy Wharton's a sleaze. You can do better than him, Katrin...and no, I'm not referring to myself."

"Oh, Luke, I'm sorry," she cried, "I shouldn't have said that. I hurt you, didn't I? I know I'm doing this all wrong. But I—"

"I sure don't like being put on a par with Guy Wharton."

"I'm not going to his room," she said rapidly. "I don't care what he tells the management, he can tell them anything he likes. I've been feeling like a caged bear for the last six months, and I'm sick to death of this job anyway. If I got fired it would be no great loss."

"A caged bear—strong language. Is that why you go sailing on the lake in a south wind?"

"Well, of course."

Luke let out his pent-up breath in a long sigh. "I'll deal with Guy. I've got enough leverage that I could ruin him if I chose to."

"I don't need your help! Let him say what he wants— I'm leaving here by the end of the summer, so why should I care? My friend Anna knows who I really am, and the rest don't matter."

"And where am I in that?"

"I've already told you," she said stonily. "Whatever my secrets are, they're nothing to do with you."

"I do wish you'd tell me," Luke said with such intensity that he was taken aback.

"Too bad."

"You're one heck of a stubborn woman!"

"If I weren't, you'd be trampling all over me."

She had a point. Taking a moment to gather his thoughts, Luke said, "Katrin, you egged Guy on in the dining room—if you were really scared of him, you wouldn't have spilled the brandy, or showed him you knew your way around the financial pages. But when he was threatening you a few minutes ago, you looked…despairing, I guess, is the closest I can get. Beaten."

The words tumbled from her lips. "Have you never had anything so awful happen to you that when you go back there, even in your imagination, all the old emotions overwhelm you? Just as they did when it was going on?" She drew a ragged breath. "Or are you immune from all that, Luke?"

As though time and space had collapsed, Luke was suddenly back in the shack at Teal Lake the day his mother had left, never to return. His father's drunken rampage, smashing glasses and crockery, the flames from the old woodstove flickering crazily over the ceiling. And in one corner, clutching an old teddy bear, cowered a little boy with black hair and dark eyes, terrified and alone.

Katrin said slowly, "So you do know what I'm talking about. What happened to you, Luke?"

With a shuddering breath, Luke hauled himself back to the present, away from an abyss that he'd fled years ago, a nightmare filled with noise and fire and unending fear. God knows what he looked like. He raked his fingers through his hair. "Nothing happened. Your imagination's working overtime."

"I don't think so." With sudden violence she cried, "What's wrong with admitting you're vulnerable? Just like the rest of the human race?"

Had he ever, wittingly or unwittingly, revealed as much

of himself to anyone else as he had to Katrin in the last few seconds? And how he hated himself—and her—for that revelation. Not knowing what else to do, Luke went on the attack. "What if Guy goes to the media? What then?"

She hugged her arms around her chest, lines of strain bracketing her mouth. "He won't. He'll be so hungover in the morning, he'll do well to get out of bed."

It was painfully obvious she was trying to convince herself as much as Luke. Luke said savagely, "In effect, he's blackmailing you."

"Don't be so melodramatic!"

"I'm telling it like I see it."

"You're overreacting," she said coldly. "Luke, I've got to go home, I'm really tired."

She looked more than tired. She looked at the end of her rope, with faint blue shadows under her eyes, her face haunted and unhappy. His only desire to comfort her, to somehow let her know that she wasn't alone with her secrets, he awkwardly rested his hand on her wrist.

She looked down. In a strange voice she said, "You have such beautiful fingers. Long and lean…"

By mutual compulsion they fell into each other's arms, Luke's hands locking around her waist, her mouth straining upward to his. Her palms were flat to his chest, burning through the fabric of his shirt; the first touch of her lips enveloped him in a tumult of desire. He thrust with his tongue, pulling her hard against his body. As she melted into him, tinder to his flame, she fumbled with the buttons on his shirt. Then, like a streak of fire, Luke felt her touch his bare chest, almost shyly, with a tiny tug at the tangled hair on his torso.

He groaned with pleasure, aching to feel her naked breasts, warm and soft and yielding against his flesh. His kiss deepened. Then he reached for the clasp that held her hair, wanting to free its silken flow over his wrist. Nibbling at her lips, he said huskily, "You should never wear your hair like this. I want to see it loose on a pillow, Katrin, I want to bury my face in it. I want you naked in my bed..."

As precipitously as she'd reached for him, Katrin pulled back. Her hands pressed to her cheeks, she whispered, "What's *wrong* with me? I'm doing it again, kissing you as though I'm in love with you, as though I can't get enough of you—oh God, I can't bear this."

In the dim light, Luke was sure he could see the glimmer of tears in her eyes. "Don't cry..."

"I'm not! Two years ago I swore I—" She stopped, aghast.

"What happened two years ago?" Luke said with dangerous quietness.

A shudder rippled through her body. Fear and pain flashed across her features so fast Luke might have imagined them. But he hadn't. They were real. Her voice cracking, she said, "If you have the slightest feeling for me, Luke, leave me alone. Go back to the resort. Go to New York, go to San Francisco, go anywhere in the world. You'll forget me by the time you arrive at the airport, I know you will—your normal life will catch up with you and take over. That's all I ask—that you forget about me."

She bit her lip, and for a moment he thought she was going to say something else. Then she struck his hands from her waist, whirled and ran away from him toward the staff parking lot, her black uniform blending into the night.

Luke took one quick step after her. Then he stopped dead. He could chase her and force his way into her car. Or he could let her go. It was his choice.

For a crazy moment that was outside of time, Luke felt as though his heart were being torn apart; as though every choice he'd ever made had been leading to this one. To a woman who'd been swallowed by the darkness. A woman with a secret.

He took a deep, harsh breath. He had no use for such fanciful guff. Woman of darkness, woman of secrets. He was losing his marbles. It was time he went back to civilization, to the sophisticated types he dated who knew the score. In fact, he was going to do precisely what Katrin had suggested: get on his plane tomorrow morning and forget all about her.

The quicker the better.

But first he had one piece of unfinished business.

Luke marched back to the lodge and took the stairs two at a time to the third floor. Then he halted outside Room 334. He tapped gently, rather as Katrin might have tapped, and waited.

Nothing happened. He knocked again, louder this time, again without result. Pressing his ear to the door, Luke could have sworn he heard a guttural snoring coming from Guy's room. So Katrin had been right; she had nothing to fear from Guy. Not tonight, anyway.

He'd make double sure of that. Taking a piece of paper from his pocket notebook, Luke scrawled a very succinct message on it, knelt down and inserted it under the door, and then headed upstairs to his suite.

Guy wouldn't be telling the management or the media anything tomorrow. Not if he valued his own skin.

If only he, Luke, could fix the turmoil in his gut as easily. Or did he mean his heart, not his gut?

Back in his own bedroom, he packed quickly, then went to stand by the window, gazing out over the black waters of the lake. If this were a story, and not real life, he'd be at the airport right now. That would be a tidy finish to an episode that had totally unsettled him. Unfortunately real life required him to get up in the morning, go to breakfast, say goodbye to his cohorts, including Guy; and face Katrin again.

Luke knew a good many swearwords, having grown up

in a rough and tumble mining town in the bush. Not one of them seemed remotely adequate to his feelings. All he hoped was that he wouldn't dream about her again. That would really be the final straw.

Luke did dream, tangled and distorted dreams in which Katrin, in a ridiculously ruffled wedding dress and her ugly glasses, was arm in arm with his father, who was equipped with snorkel gear and the financial section of the newspaper. Then Katrin and Guy were out on the tarmac accompanied by a trio of Icelandic ponies draped in peasant skirts. Katrin was jeering at Luke as he boarded his plane. He woke with that ugly laughter echoing in his ears.

He rubbed his eyes. At least she'd been wearing clothes; another night of erotic dreams would have finished him off. He had no idea what the dream was trying to tell him, or why Guy was in it. But he'd stake his bottom dollar that Guy was nothing to Katrin. She was genuine, every emotion she'd ever shown Luke coming straight from her heart.

Not that this made any difference.

Luke climbed out of bed, restlessly working the muscles in his bare shoulders. The best thing in this whole mess was her advice. Forget me, she'd said. And he had every intention of doing so, just as soon as he could.

If he pushed it, he could leave the resort in an hour and a half. Go for it, Luke, he thought, and headed for the shower. He checked out on his way to the dining room, leaving his bag at the front desk, and took his seat at the table. The young man called Stan was pouring Rupert's coffee. With an uncomfortable mingling of relief and pure rage, Luke saw that Katrin was taking someone's order over by the far wall.

She'd gotten her tables changed so that she wouldn't have to talk to him.

We'll see about that, thought Luke, and asked for black

coffee. When he'd finished eating, he said a quick round of goodbyes and crossed the width of the room. Katrin was gathering the used dishes from one of her tables. He stopped beside it, aware that several people were within earshot, and said pleasantly, "I just wanted to say goodbye, Katrin, and thank you for everything you've done all week." A statement that should leave plenty to her imagination.

She straightened, holding a heap of dirty plates; she looked as though she'd had as little sleep as he had. She said politely, "Goodbye, sir. Have a safe journey."

Her eyes didn't look polite. Far from it. He said, "I've already told you you're wasted as a waitress—you're far too intelligent. You should leave here, go to a city and get a job more suited to your IQ. Go to New York, for instance. Or to San Francisco."

Her breath hissed between her teeth; her fingers tightened around the pile of plates. He added softly, "I dare you. To throw them at me, I mean."

"That might jeopardize my tip, sir," she said, giving him a brilliant, insincere smile. "And now, if you'll excuse me, I have work to do."

"Goodbye, Katrin," Luke said; and heard, to his inner fury, the edge in his voice. The hint of rawness that said, more clearly than words, that this was no ordinary goodbye.

He turned on his heel, nodded at a couple of Italians and left the dining room. It was an anticlimactic ending to an episode as inconclusive as it had been unnerving: his last contact with a woman who had aroused him sexually and emotionally in ways he could only deplore.

Temporary madness. That's all it was. And the cure? To get as far away from here as he could and never come back.

To forget Katrin Sigurdson. Her beauty and laughter, her adventurous spirit and her independence. Her body. Her unspoken secrets.

To get his life back on track. Where it belonged.

Luke picked up his bag from the front desk and went outdoors to the parking lot. As he drove toward the road, his back to the resort and the glimmering lake, he told himself he was glad to be leaving. Of course he was.

He'd worked very hard to construct his life. He wasn't going to allow a blue-eyed blonde, no matter how beautiful, to disrupt it.

And that was that.

CHAPTER EIGHT

FIVE days after he'd left the resort, Luke parked his sleek silver sportscar in the garage of his ultramodern house in Pacific Heights, and went inside. As always when he'd been away, he was struck by how impersonal and stark the rooms were, with their angled white walls, designer furniture, and the cold gleam of highly polished parquet. Not for the first time, he thought he should sell the house.

What had possessed him to buy it in the first place?

To show that he'd arrived, he thought dryly. That Luke MacRae from Teal Lake had a prestigious address in San Francisco, a city many considered America's most beautiful. And, of course, to cut any last ties with Teal Lake. No one from there would have lived in a cement and glass box painted white and trimmed with metal.

He'd outgrown the house; which had nothing to do with its vast floorspace. What he should do is purchase some land outside the city and build a house out of cedar and stone, with a view of the beach and the rolling surf of the Pacific. Yeah, he thought. He might just do that. He'd check out the acreages that were available, and find an architect who dealt in anything other than postmodern.

Luke opened the mail, turned on his computer to scan his emails, and listened to the four messages on his telephone; three were from women he'd dated. Then he wandered over to the huge expanse of plate glass in the living room and gazed out. Another reason he'd bought the house was for the spectacular view of the city. Sailboats dotted the turquoise waters of the bay; the distant hills were a misty, cloud-shadowed blue. It was midafternoon. He should go to his office headquarters, housed in the elegant spire of the Transamerica Pyramid. Show his face and make sure everything was ticking over the way he liked.

There'd been no messages from Katrin.

How could there be? For one thing, she didn't have his address; for another, she had no reason to get in touch with him and every reason not to.

So far, he hadn't succeeded in forgetting her.

He'd gone out with two different women in New York, both ambitious and successful women, each of whom had let him know she'd be happy to warm his bed.

He hadn't asked. Because neither had made him laugh like Katrin? Because each took the expensive dinner, and the waitress who served it, for granted? Because he couldn't care less if he ever saw either of them again?

He could get a date for this evening, if he wanted one. Go dancing in one of the clubs south of Market, find a jazz bar, or see what was playing at the Geary Theater. If he tried, he could probably even find someone to play Frisbee with him on Ocean Beach.

And it was then that Luke remembered the three photos he'd taken of Katrin playing Frisbee by the lake with Lara and Tomas. He'd get them developed. That's what he'd do.

As he was unlocking his suitcase, the telephone rang. He grabbed the receiver. "Hello?"

"Luke, Ramon here. I wasn't sure if you were back today or tomorrow."

Again Luke was aware of a crushing and utterly illogical disappointment that the person on the other end wasn't Katrin. Get a life, Luke MacRae. "Hi, Ramon," he said, "I just got in half an hour ago. It was a good conference, I made some useful contacts. How've you been?"

Ramon Torres was a high-ranking police officer whom Luke had met several years ago at the indoor tennis club he belonged to. On the court, they were more or less evenly matched, Ramon with a tendency to an erratic brilliance, Luke somewhat stronger and more consistent. From a series of hard-fought games, they'd moved gradually and naturally to an undemanding friendship. At least every two weeks they had lunch together, sparring over politics, learning from each other's areas of expertise; occasionally Luke had dinner with Ramon, his wife Rosita and their three children. Somehow, over the years, it had become clear that both men had pulled themselves upward from backgrounds of poverty and deprivation: Luke from Teal Lake, Ramon from the slums of Mexico City. They never spoke directly about this. But it was there, an unspoken bond between two laconic men.

"I've got a court booked at noon tomorrow," Ramon said. "Want a game? We could have lunch afterward, if you've got time."

"Sure. Sounds like a good idea. As always at these shindigs, I ate too much... I'll meet you there."

They rang off. Luke changed into casual clothes and drove downtown to the nearest camera shop. The prints would be ready the next morning; he could pick them up on his way to the tennis club.

So at eleven-forty the next morning, Luke walked out of the shop with an unopened envelope in his hand. He got in his car, drove to the club, and parked a little distance away from all the other cars. It was one of those summer days of thick fog, a heavy white blanket spread over the city, cooling the air.

Appropriate, thought Luke, realizing he was reluctant to open the envelope. He'd been in a fog ever since he'd left Manitoba. Oh, at his meetings in New York he'd functioned at top efficiency, and he was doing the same at the office here; there was nothing new about that. But the rest of the time he felt as though his feet weren't quite on the ground. As though part of him was still back in Askja.

His normal life had taken over; but he hadn't forgotten Katrin. Far from it.

She was even more real to him here, hundreds of miles away, than she'd been at the resort, Luke thought, tugging at the tape on the flap of the envelope. He had the eerie sense that if he turned around quickly enough, she'd be standing there, her brilliant blue eyes gazing straight at him.

Ridiculous. Get a grip. He didn't need a woman turning his life upside down, he reminded himself. Not now or ever.

With sudden decision Luke pulled the flap open, took out the prints and leafed through them. His heart jumped in his chest. There she was, on the beach, her hair swirling around her head, her slim legs bare to the sun as she reached for the Frisbee. In the other two photos she was laughing, Tomas grinning back at her, their shadows striping the sand.

She looked young and carefree, and very beautiful.

He shoved the photos in his gym bag and hurried into the club. He was late. He was never late.

Ramon was tossing balls into the air and practising his serves when Luke joined him on the court. *"Buenos días, amigo,"* Ramon said. His gaze sharpened. "You okay?"

Luke should have remembered Ramon had a law officer's ability to assess people with just a glance. "Sure," he said, jogging on the spot to warm up. "Want to rally for a few minutes?"

What would Ramon have thought of Katrin in her shapeless uniform and ugly glasses? Would he have discerned the woman of passion—and secrets—behind her disguise? Or would he have been as obtuse as Luke had been?

Grimly Luke forced himself to concentrate. They rallied for five minutes, then settled into the game. But Luke's focus was off. He lost the first set 6-4, won the second by sheer brute force, and lost the final set 6-2. He and Ramon headed for the locker room, showered, then walked to a little Greek restaurant they both liked. Once they'd ordered, Ramon said, "What's up, Luke? Was business off-kilter for you up there in the wilds of Canada?"

"It went fine."

"You've never played so badly before."

"Thanks," Luke said dryly. "How's Rosita? And the family?"

Rosita, Ramon's gorgeous and flamboyant wife, had had three children since their marriage, and to everyone's surprise, including her own, settled into motherhood as though made for it. "She's in decorating mode," Ramon said, wiping the froth from his beer off his moustache. "Tearing the rooms apart, painting up a storm. The kids are fine. Usually covered in paint by the time I get home. So you don't want to tell me what's wrong."

"I met this woman," Luke blurted.

"About time."

"Marriage isn't for everyone, Ramon," Luke said forcefully. "One of these years I'll settle down. But until then, I like playing the field."

"This woman...she wanted marriage?"

"No."

Ramon smiled at the waitress as she put his spanakopita in front of him. "So," he said amiably, once they were alone again, "she was immune to your charm and your undoubted good looks?"

"Yeah. Well, no. Sort of. I guess."

Ramon gave him a quizzical look. "One thing I've always admired about you is your decisiveness. Yes. No. Always you know which one to choose. Except now."

"It's not that simple," Luke said edgily. "She wasn't one of the delegates. She was working as a waitress at the resort."

Ramon raised his brows. "So she was after your money? I thought you were used to that by now."

"She wasn't! I swear she wasn't."

"You went to bed with her?"

Luke ate a black olive. "I feel like I'm in the dock," he said, scowling. "No, I did not."

"But you wanted to. Some women say no just to keep a man interested. On the hook."

"She wasn't like that."

"You've got it bad, *amigo,*" Ramon chuckled. "She was beautiful, yes?"

"Oh, yeah, she was beautiful." Luke frowned. "She reminded me of someone, but I can't think who. And she had a thing about San Francisco, reacted like a startled deer every time it was mentioned."

"What was her name?"

"Katrin." Impulsively Luke fumbled in his gym bag, took out the envelope of prints and passed the three of Katrin across the table. Ramon took them carefully by the corners, his total attention focussed on the laughing woman on the beach. When he looked up, he was no longer smiling.

"What's her last name?" he asked in a clipped voice.

"Sigurdson. What's the matter?"

"Sigurdson…that's right. Although I knew her as Katrin Staines. Widow of Donald Staines. That mean anything to you?"

Luke's nerves tightened like overstretched wire. Katrin a widow? He said brusquely, "Not a damn thing—and I have a pretty good memory for names. What do you mean, you knew her? When? And where? And who was this Donald Staines?"

"There's no easy way to tell you this," Ramon said. "She used to live in San Francisco. About two and a half years ago, her husband was murdered."

"Murdered?" Luke repeated dazedly. "Are you sure we're talking about the same woman?"

Ramon flicked the photos with his finger. "I recognized her immediately...she's not exactly forgettable. It came out at the trial that she was of Icelandic descent, from northern Canada. I don't forget these details, it's part of my job."

"Trial?" Luke said sharply. "What trial?"

"She had a motive. Money. A great deal of money. The prosecution made the most of that, of course. But she also had an ironclad alibi. In the end, although they did their best to suggest she hired someone to kill Donald Staines, they couldn't make it stick. There was absolutely no record of her paying out any large sums of money in the preceding few months."

Luke stared at his companion, his brain whirling. "Am I dreaming?" he demanded. "Are we actually sitting here having this conversation?"

"Unfortunately, yes."

Out of the blue, Luke was transported back to Askja on his last evening there. Under the birch trees, Guy had said something to Katrin that had made her sag with despair. What exactly had he said? It had had to do with a stain on her reputation.

Her married name had been Staines.

So that was why she'd looked so upset. And no wonder she'd reacted so strongly to any mention of San Francisco, the city where she'd lived; where her trial had taken place.

He said at random, "I was out of the country for several months two years ago. But I must have seen a photo in the newspaper, and that's why I had that strange feeling that I recognized her."

"Are you in love with her?" Ramon asked very quietly.

"No. Of course not! But it's a shock, nevertheless." Trying to gather his scattered wits, Luke ploughed on. "You know, I'm listening to every word that you're saying.

Words like *murder* and *trial* and *alibi*. But I can't connect them with the woman I know. I just can't. I keep thinking there must be a mistake. Or this is some kind of sick joke."

"Not on my part," Ramon said pithily.

Luke gave him a rueful smile. "Sorry, you know I didn't mean you. You've knocked me sideways, that's all."

"I can see that… Why are you so sure that the Katrin you know couldn't have murdered her husband? Who by all accounts was a very nasty piece of work."

Scarcely aware of what he was doing, Luke buttered a piece of crusty white bread. "She couldn't have. The woman I met at that resort wasn't capable of murder." He gave a baffled laugh. "I know that's not a rational response. But that's the way I see it. Dammit, I know I'm right."

"Ah," said Ramon. "How very interesting."

"Don't play games with me, Ramon."

"I'm not. But I'm glad you said what you did. Rather than asking me if I thought she was guilty."

"Guilty of murder? *Katrin?* I don't care what the prosecution said, Katrin Sigurdson couldn't possibly have killed her husband. And to say she hired someone else to do it is laughable. There's not an underhanded bone in that woman's body—her honesty was one of the things that first attracted me to her. Even if I didn't always like being at the receiving end."

Ramon took a healthy bite of spanakopita. His mouth full, he mumbled, "Her alibi was real. She was with friends overnight, and the murder happened in the small hours of the morning. But she most certainly had a motive, and that was what caused the most difficulty."

"Okay," Luke said, tension hardening his jaw. "So now I'll ask you the question. Do *you* think she did it?"

"Nope. Never did. I have very good radar for liars, and she wasn't anywhere near my screen. But her motive…she and Donald Staines had had a huge fight that evening. The servants heard it, and she freely admitted to it. He was a wealthy man, and—this is off the record, my friend—the scum of the earth. As well as being an unfaithful husband he was an embezzler, not to mention a highflyer in some very dubious circles.''

Ramon paused to take a long pull at his beer. "Eat up, Luke," he added, a smile crinkling the lines around his eyes. "I want you in better shape for our next game."

Luke's heartbeat had finally settled down to normal; but his hands were cold, and he still hadn't quite taken in that this was Katrin they were talking about. Manfully he took a mouthful of salad.

"During the course of their disagreement, Katrin told her husband she was leaving him. That very evening. He said he'd cut her out of his will first thing the next morning if she did so. She said go right ahead, she couldn't care less...then she left the house by taxi with the clothes she was standing up in, and went to her friends' house. They were a highly respected couple, he was a chief attorney, she was a hospital administrator. The three of them stayed up most of the night, talking."

"A cast-iron alibi," Luke said thoughtfully.

"Indeed. In my opinion, the case was mishandled from the start. It should never have gone to trial. But it had too many of the right ingredients: money, corruption, scandal, and a beautiful woman as the defendant. When you put all that together with murder and a possible hit man, you can imagine what happened. The press had a field day."

Belatedly Luke's brain was now working at top speed. "So that would explain why Katrin buried herself in Askja. There are no major newspapers there. And who would connect a waitress with Katrin Staines?"

"Not you. Obviously."

Guy had. But Katrin hadn't really cared. She'd been

ready to leave Askja anyway. "What a terrible ordeal for anyone to go through," Luke said.

"I felt very sorry for her. She had enormous dignity and courage...both before and during the trial. But you could see it wearing her down, day by day, month by month. By the time it was over, she was on the verge of collapse. She got her lawyers to sell the house, packed her bags and left town. I lost track of her after that. But every now and then I'd wonder what had happened to her."

Briefly Luke described Katrin's situation. "She's ready to leave Askja," he finished. "But I can't imagine she'd ever come back here."

"Not unless she had a reason to," Ramon said, his eyes twinkling.

"Don't go there," Luke said harshly.

"Warning me off?"

"You said it." Then Luke grimaced. "I haven't asked the obvious question. Did they ever find out who did murder Donald Staines?"

"Case unsolved." It was Ramon's turn to frown. "And you know how I love those."

Luke dug into his salad. Ramon was his closest friend, but right now he needed to be by himself. Alone. So he could think. Take in all the implications of what he'd learned.

Half an hour later, after settling on a time for their next game, the two men parted in the parking lot of the sports club.

Luke walked toward his car, his gym bag in his hand. For the space of ten minutes he sat in the car, staring straight ahead at the brick wall.

His lunch with Ramon had cleared up so many unanswered questions, things he hadn't understood about Katrin. He now knew why she lived in a remote village, worked at a job that in no way fulfilled her potential, and was wary of wealthy men. She had very good reasons; furthermore, after an ordeal that must have tested her to the limits, she'd had the sense to retreat and lick her wounds.

He couldn't bear to think of her going through a protracted trial conducted in full gaze of the press and the public. Living day after day with flashbulbs bursting in her face, the prosecution ascribing to her things she would never have contemplated, the ceaseless and remorseless prying into her private life; add to that the terror she must have felt that justice might miscarry and she be held responsible for something she hadn't done...

He banged his palm on the steering wheel. No wonder she'd looked so utterly despairing when Guy had confronted her that night.

Wishing he could take on Ramon in the tennis court right now and get rid of some of his pent-up energy, Luke looked around him. The fog had lifted; the car was starting to warm up. So what was he going to do? Go back to work?

He had no reason not to. Perhaps now that he knew Katrin's secret, he could forget about her. For hadn't that tantalizing air of mystery been one of the things that had drawn him to her? That, along with all the contradictions that had now been so neatly explained.

Where would she go when she left Askja? Return to the States? Stay in Canada? And how would she earn her living?

Hadn't she inherited her husband's money? But if so, why was she working as a waitress?

His jaw set, Luke put the key in the ignition. None of these questions was any of his concern. The resort in Askja and his brief sojourn there were history. Over and done with. Along with the woman who had caused him, briefly, to forget all his hard-won control.

Luke turned left out of the parking lot, toward the distant spire of the Transamerica Pyramid, the city's tallest building and a notable landmark. Once he got there, he must phone Andreas in Greece.

That was the final piece of unfinished business from the mining conference at the Askja resort.

CHAPTER NINE

FOUR days later, Luke was on a flight to Manitoba.

He'd made a phone call before he left, to book his room at the resort. Very casually he'd said, near the end of the conversation, "I'd like a table in the dining room with the same waitress I had before... I believe her name was Katrin." And then waited, with a dry mouth, to be told she no longer worked there.

"No problem at all, sir. We'll see you tomorrow evening."

It was seven-thirty that evening by the time Luke climbed out of his rental car at the resort. He took a deep breath of the cool air. He could smell the lake. The trees rustled companionably behind him. He felt simultaneously very tired and totally wired.

He was here. In only a few minutes, he'd see Katrin again.

Beyond that, he couldn't go. He didn't know why he was here, or what he was going to say to her; nor did he have any idea how she'd react to his presence.

He wanted to make love to her. That much hadn't changed.

Grabbing his overnight bag, he walked to the lobby, checked in and went to his suite. He took a quick shower and dressed in casual cotton trousers and a short-sleeved shirt, combing his hair into some kind of order. He should have gotten a hair cut, he thought absently. His heart was racing, as though he'd been jogging. He felt about as suave as a twelve-year-old.

In the lobby, he grabbed the daily paper; he needed

something to do with his hands. Or somewhere to hide his face. He'd never thought of himself as a coward.

What was he doing here?

He'd come on impulse, after that equally impulsive visit to the library in San Francisco yesterday afternoon, where he'd read the reports of the trial. Or had he come because he couldn't forget Katrin, no matter what he did?

He'd tried. For two whole days, after his lunch with Ramon, he'd pushed any thoughts of her out of his mind as soon as they surfaced.

Forty-eight hours. It didn't seem like much.

On Saturday night he'd even had dinner with a tall brunette, an architect from Sausalito. A move that had proved equally ineffective.

Taking a deep breath, Luke walked into the dining room. Olaf, the maître d', said politely, "Good evening, sir. Let me show you to your table."

Luke was given a table by the window, which gave him a view of the wharf and of a daysailer bobbing gently in the breeze, its red sail furled. He buried his nose in the wine list.

Then, as though a magnet had drawn his attention, he looked up. Katrin was crossing the dining room, carrying a loaded tray, her attention on the table nearest his. He noticed immediately that she was no longer wearing her ugly plastic glasses; her hair was in a loose and very becoming knot on the back of her head, a few strands curling on her nape. Then he saw how pale and tired she looked. Dispirited, he thought slowly. Sad. What could be wrong?

Just before she put the tray down, she glanced over at his table. For a moment frozen in time, she stood like a statue, staring right at him as if he were a ghost. The color fled from her cheeks. The tray tilted sideways; the loaded plates slid gently and inexorably toward the edge.

She suddenly realized what was happening and shifted

her grip in a valiant effort to straighten the tray. But she was too late. One after another, four platefuls of roast beef with all the trimmings inscribed graceful arcs in the air and landed on the carpet, the food with an uncouth squelch, the plates with a loud clatter. A Yorkshire pudding rolled under the table, coming to rest by a guest's sandal. The broccoli, Luke noticed, was the same shade as the carpet.

There was a moment of dead silence. If Katrin's cheeks a moment ago had been white as paper, they were now as red as the sails on her boat. She put the empty tray down on the dumbwaiter and looked helplessly at the congealed mass of gravy and rare roast beef at her feet. It was quite clear that she had no idea what to do next.

Luke stood up. Into the silence he said, "You didn't hurt your wrist?"

His voice sounded like it was coming from another man, one who had nothing to do with him. Discovering that his one urge was to pick her up, carry her bodily out of the room and put her on the first plane to San Francisco, he added without any tact whatsoever, "You don't look so hot...what's the matter?"

"What are you doing here?" Katrin croaked.

She'd asked the one question to which, basically, he didn't have an answer. As he sought for words, Olaf arrived on the scene with two waiters in tow, equipped with brooms, cloths and a pail of soapy water.

"Our apologies, ladies and gentlemen," Olaf said smoothly to the four people whose roast beef was on the floor rather than on the table, and who had been listening in fascinated silence to the exchange between Katrin and Luke. "Your meals will be replaced as quickly as possible," he went on, "and they will be, of course, compliments of the chef." Subtly his voice changed. "Katrin, perhaps you could take the plates back to the kitchen and reorder immediately...Katrin?"

She gave Luke a hunted look, then bent to pick up the plates. Plunking them on the empty tray, she almost ran across the dining room. As throughout the room the hum of conversation resumed, Olaf and his crew cleaned up the mess with remarkable efficiency. Then Olaf walked over to Luke's table. "Perhaps I could take your order, sir?"

Luke hadn't even looked at the menu. "Soup of the day and whatever fresh fish you have," he said.

"Wine, sir?"

"Perrier, thanks." He needed all his wits about him if he was going to talk to Katrin tonight. He should have phoned her yesterday evening and told her he was coming. But deep down he'd been afraid that if he did so, she'd vanish.

Very soon one of the waiters brought the second round of roast beef, passing a plate to each of the four guests. Then Katrin came out of the kitchen carrying Luke's soup. She walked straight toward him. With a quiver of inner laughter, Luke could tell that she'd progressed from shock and embarrassment to rage. All her movements jerky, like a wind-up toy, she put a basket of rolls on his table and the bowl of soup. Spinach soup, by the look of it. He'd never liked spinach.

He supposed it served him right. He said, trying not to sound overly familiar, and as a result sounding indifferent, "I'm sorry I startled you."

Between her teeth, she gritted, "Why are you here?"

"To see you," Luke said.

Her lashes flickered. Once again her cheeks paled, until they matched the white linen cloth on his table. She whispered, "You know. About Donald. Don't you?"

"You didn't do it," Luke said, putting all the force he could behind his words. "You were totally innocent. I knew that the moment I heard about it."

"I inherited all his money," she said flatly.

"I don't care if you inherited a billion dollars—you had nothing to do with his death."

To his horror Luke saw tears flood Katrin's eyes and tremble on her lashes. "Oh God," she said, "I've got to get out of here."

With a huge effort Luke stayed sitting in his chair, his fingers wrapped like manacles around the arms. "I'm really sorry," he said, and this time could hear the emotion in his voice. "Taking you by surprise like this was about the dumbest move I could have made."

She drew a long, shaky breath. "For once we're in complete agreement."

"Well, that's something. And now you'd better go back to the kitchen... Olaf's glaring at me. He probably thinks we're having a rip-roaring affair."

"There's not a chance in the world of that," she retorted with a trace of her usual spirit. Then she pivoted and hurried back to the kitchen, ignoring Olaf as if he were just one more oak chair.

Hoping she didn't mean it, Luke buttered a slice of crusty French bread and took the first mouthful of soup. It smelled like and tasted of spinach. Naturally. Trying to think of it as penance, he unfolded his newspaper.

Why had Katrin been so shaken up by her first sight of him?

The fish was excellent. He followed it with a maple syrup mousse that more than made up for the soup, and two cups of coffee. After she'd poured the second one, Katrin said politely, "Can I get you anything else, sir?"

The four guests who'd had the roast beef had just left. Luke said forthrightly, "Can I meet you somewhere after work? Do you have your car here?"

"My bike. Why do you want to meet me?"

"I need to talk to you!"

She looked at him coldly, rather as if he were a fly she'd

just discovered in his spinach soup. "You came all this way to talk to me? You expect me to believe that?"

"Yes, I did. And yes, I do."

"I'd have thought you had better things to do with your time. More profitable, anyway."

"I came here to see you, Katrin," Luke repeated, his voice rising in spite of himself.

"Short of hiring a bouncer, I'm not going to get rid of you, am I?"

"Not before you and I sit down and discuss everything I found out."

"You're boxing me in!"

"I know I'm not doing this right," Luke said in exasperation. "Please, Katrin, let me come to your place later on, will you do that much?"

For a moment it hung in the balance. Then she snapped, "No earlier than ten-thirty."

Her eyes were now filled with a mixture of hostility and terror; Luke wasn't sure which he disliked more. "I'll be there," he said. "Tell Olaf to jump in the lake if he gives you a hard time."

"My pay gets docked the price of four plates of roast beef," she said. *"C'est la vie."*

"That's disgraceful—the resort shouldn't be allowed to get away with it."

"I'm not a labor lawyer," Katrin said sweetly, "I'm a stockbroker. See you later."

Somehow—once again—Luke was quite sure she was telling the truth. Guy had known her background; that's why he'd goaded her with talk about investments. She'd be very good at her job, Luke would be willing to bet. Although most people might steer clear of a beautiful female broker who had a murder trial in her past.

Had he really categorized her as deadly dull the first time

he'd laid eyes on her? He couldn't have been more off base if he'd tried.

It was five to nine. He had an hour and a half to kill.

He went for a stroll along the lakeshore, listening to the shrill chorus of frogs and the soft lap of waves on the sand, the hands on his watch moving with agonizing slowness. He should have been on a jet to Whitehorse today, to look after a contract dispute; instead he'd delegated the job. Early this morning he ought to have been talking to a foreman in Texas. But yesterday afternoon had put paid to all his plans and schedules. Yesterday afternoon he'd gone to the library.

Against his better judgment Luke had spent a couple of hours there, reading through the accounts of the trial. The flash photos of Katrin had cut him to the heart. Her dark suit and silk shirt, her smooth, sophisticated chignon, her elegant pumps and gold jewellery: none of these were familiar to him, showing him another side to a woman who was still, in her essence, mysterious. But her air of reserve and her pride of bearing came across even in the grainy newsprint; these he knew all too well.

The headlines were cheap and degrading; her privacy had been mercilessly invaded for months at a time. As for her dead husband, Luke loathed him on sight, with his heavy jowls and thin, rapacious mouth. Why on earth had Katrin married him?

Even now, on the lakeshore, Luke couldn't get those photos out of his mind.

At ten twenty-four he was in the parking lot unlocking his car. At precisely ten twenty-nine he turned into Katrin's driveway. The lights were on in the house. A bicycle was parked by the side door. He walked up the steps, wiped his damp palms down the sides of his trousers, and rang the doorbell.

The door was pulled open immediately. Katrin ushered

him in and shut the door with an aggressive snap. Then she stood a careful three feet away from him and said brusquely, "We can't talk for long. I'm on the breakfast shift."

As an opener, thought Luke, this wasn't encouraging. She looked as though she'd just gotten out of the shower, her hair still in its loose knot, damp strands curling by her ears. Her cheeks were pink, her eyes guarded; her jeans and loose sweater hadn't been chosen with seduction in mind. He said, "I like your hair like that."

"You didn't come here to talk about my hair."

He said calmly, "May I sit down?"

She flushed. "Do you want something to drink?"

"No, thanks." He looked around, trying to get a sense of her surroundings. He was standing in an old-fashioned kitchen, panelled in pine, with colorful woven rugs on the softwood floor and plants on the wide sills. There were dishes in the sink, papers on the oak table, mail thrown on the counter. It was a room as different from his immaculately tidy stainless steel kitchen as could be imagined. He pulled out a chair and sat down at the table. With obvious reluctance, Katrin sat down across from him.

As far away from him as she could get.

Luke cleared his throat and said the first thing that came into his head. "Why did you drop the plates when you saw me?"

"You were the last person I was expecting to see."

"Come on, Katrin, there was more to it than that."

"If you just came up here to interrogate me," she said tautly, "you can turn right around and go back."

He leaned forward. "Yesterday I went through all the newspaper accounts of the trial... I can't imagine how you survived such an ordeal."

She tilted her chin. "I knew I was innocent and I had the support of good friends."

This wasn't going the way he'd hoped. Hadn't he pictured her falling into his arms as soon as she opened the door? "Why did you marry him?" Luke asked quietly.

"For his money, of course."

Luke held hard to his temper. "I don't believe you."

"Then you're one of the few."

"I never did like going along with the crowd," he said with a crooked smile, trying to lighten the atmosphere.

"I was young. Naive, if you're feeling charitable. Stupid, if you're not."

She was scowling down at the table, digging at the grain in the wood with one fingernail, the light from the Tiffany lamp shining on her wheat-gold hair. Wanting her so badly he could taste it, Luke said, "I don't mean to be interrogating you—you've had more than enough of that. But after I saw those photos of you in the papers—your dignity and courage, the strain in your face—I can't explain it. I booked a flight and here I am. I should have let you know, I guess. But I figured if I did, you might take off."

"You were right. I probably would have."

"Why?"

"We've got nothing to say to each other."

He suddenly reached across the table and stilled her restless fingers. She snatched her hand back. "Don't touch me!"

Pain knifed him; followed by jealousy, hot and imperative, clawing at his entrails. "You've got me out of your system, haven't you?" he snarled. "Who with, Katrin?"

She glared at him. "There's one thing you should know about me, Luke MacRae—I don't have affairs."

Slowly his body relaxed. "I've dated three different women since I left here and they all bored me to tears."

"Hurray for you."

"Why did you marry him?" Luke repeated.

For a long moment she gazed at him across the table. "If I tell you, will you go away?"

His eyes met hers, refusing to drop. "I'm not making any promises."

"You only want me because I'm not falling into your arms!"

"Give me a little more credit than that."

"I don't know what makes you tick—how could I? You're an enigma to me."

"You know you're important enough that I flew all the way up here once I found out what your secret was," Luke said forcefully. "And if you don't have affairs, Katrin, I don't chase women who don't want me around. Neither do I indulge in bed-hopping, it's not to my taste." His throat tight, he asked the second crucial question. "Do you still want to go to bed with me? Because in New York and San Francisco I couldn't forget you, day or night. Although the nights were worse. I should be in the Yukon right now dealing with contract negotiations—but I'm here instead." He gave a wintry smile. "I don't neglect business for anyone. You should be flattered."

"You frighten me," she whispered. "You're like a rock-slide—nothing in your path will stop you. And that includes me."

He was losing, Luke thought, his mouth dry. And how could he push himself on a woman whose boundaries had been cruelly invaded by police, lawyers and the avaricious appetites of the public? Not to mention her husband. "Katrin, let's get a couple of things straight," he said in a clipped voice—a voice that belonged to a high-powered businessman rather than a man attempting seduction. "Yes, I want to go to bed with you. But I'm not the marrying kind. No commitments, no permanence. In other words, I won't hang around pestering you."

"We already discussed that," she said frostily. "I'm

thinking of going to law school, so I don't want any complications in my personal life.''

Luke thoroughly disliked being seen as a complication. He said flatly, ''Right now, if you tell me you really don't want me anymore, I'll leave and I won't come back.''

His words echoed in his ears. Did he mean them? Could he do it—simply leave, and never know exactly what Katrin meant to him? Surely she did still want him, just as badly as he wanted her? She couldn't have changed that quickly, not in the few days that he'd been away. So he was now trusting her innate honesty; gambling that she'd tell him the truth.

She said evenly, ''You mean that, don't you?''

Luke nodded, reminded of that long ago day when he was negotiating for his first mine. When his whole life had lain in the balance.

Ridiculous, he told himself. We're talking bed here. Seduction. Nothing else.

And waited for her reply.

CHAPTER TEN

KATRIN said without a trace of emotion in her voice, "Yes, Luke, I still want you. That's why all that roast beef went flying. I hadn't been able to get you out of my mind and then there you were. Sitting at one of my tables."

His breath hissed between his teeth. "I knew I could count on you to be truthful."

She said rapidly, "I'll tell you why I married Donald...why I made the worst mistake in my whole life. If you still want to hear about it."

"Of course I do. That's what I came here for."

"I was born in Toronto," she said. "My father left when I was seven. I still don't know why, my mother would never talk about it. She was heartbroken. A few months later she got very sick and she died. Young as I was, I knew she didn't want to go on living without him. I was brought to Askja to live with Great-aunt Gudrun...other than Uncle Erik she was my only remaining relative, and he was hardly suitable as a surrogate parent for a little girl just turned seven."

So Katrin's father had run away from his family responsibilities, just as Luke's mother had from hers. Not that Luke was going to tell Katrin that. "Go on," he said softly.

"At first I hated it here. We'd lived in the heart of the city and all of a sudden I was living in a village where everyone knew everyone else and there wasn't as much as a toy shop." Her smile was rueful. "But my great-aunt was patient and kind, and gradually I came to love the place...she died when I was seventeen, and left me this house."

"You came back to your roots."

For the first time since he'd arrived, Katrin smiled. "Yes, I did. But I wanted more than my Icelandic heritage—I wanted to know about my father. He left here when he was young, after a fight with his father, who was Great-aunt Gudrun's elder brother. He never got in touch with his parents again, and they knew nothing about where he'd gone. After my great-aunt died, I tried to trace him. Eventually I discovered he'd died just the year before, picking grapes in the Napa Valley in California."

"So you went there."

She nodded. "I found out very little. He was a wanderer, never stayed long at any job. He had no friends and no money. So I guess he'll always remain a stranger to me...it was while I was searching through some old records in San Francisco that I met Donald."

Wishing he'd accepted her offer of a drink, Luke waited for her to continue. She said in a rush, "It's such a trite story. Donald was years older than me, and I was, of course, looking for a father figure. Classic, isn't it? Besides, I was alone in a strange country, and he could be very charming when he chose. I fell in love. Or thought I did. We were married, I trained to be a broker, and for a while everything was more or less okay. I was very busy, first as a junior in a big firm, then moving to a better position in another firm, you know how it goes. But busy as I was, I couldn't be oblivious forever. Gradually I realized Donald was being unfaithful to me. Not just once, but on a regular basis. But even worse than that were the people he'd bring into the house. His friends and business associates. Men I didn't want to be in the same room with."

Again she dug at the table with her nail. "Well, you know the rest. Things went from bad to worse, especially after he informed me he had no intention of changing his ways. Then one night we had this blazing row. I told him

I was leaving him, he threatened to cut me out of his will, and I left.''

"So he still wanted you as his wife."

"I guess so. I was good cover, being so trustworthy and respectable."

"Don't be bitter, Katrin," Luke said gently.

"You don't know how angry I've been at myself for being so trusting for so long. Anyway, after I left the house I went straight to Susan and Robert's. Thank goodness I did that. I still shudder to think what might have happened if I hadn't had that alibi."

So did he. "It's a tribute to you that you had such good friends…are you still in touch with them?"

"We write regularly. They moved to Maryland last year."

So he couldn't suggest she come to San Francisco to visit her friends Susan and Robert. "I can't believe I didn't meet you somewhere in the city during those years," Luke said.

"I kept a very low profile. First I was studying like a fiend, then I started dissociating myself from Donald and his friends." She shrugged restlessly. "I should have left him months before I did. But one of my great-aunt's precepts was to believe the best of everyone until you had evidence to the contrary. I guess I kept looking for the best in Donald. He wasn't altogether bad—he could be very witty, and not unkind, as long as I didn't interfere with his plans."

"Not much of an endorsement," Luke said dryly. He wanted to ask what sex had been like for her; and found he couldn't get his tongue around the words. He was jealous, he thought incredulously. Jealous of a dead man.

She said in a low voice, "I finally found out about his ventures on the wrong side of the law, and that was the end of it. I should never have married him! But even now, I hate to think of the way he died. That someone hated him enough to kill him.''

''You're a good woman, Katrin,'' Luke said.

''Not really,'' she muttered. ''When I came back here, I felt so battered and ashamed. I couldn't tell people about the trial, I just wanted to put it behind me. So all I said was that I was widowed. Only Anna knows the real truth.'' She ducked her head. ''I lied, in effect.''

''You looked after yourself,'' Luke said strongly. ''The trial was no one else's business.''

''I suppose.'' Picking at a loose thread in the sleeve of her sweater, her eyes downcast, Katrin said in a strangled voice, ''So now what do we do, Luke?''

The sixty-four-thousand-dollar question. ''Have you made love with anyone other than Donald?''

She shook her head. ''I've been wary of men ever since I left San Francisco. And on Askja, there's not a whole lot of choice.''

Knowing he was ridiculously pleased by her answer, making no move to touch her, Luke said, ''I've got a suggestion. Hear me out and think about it before you reply.''

She nodded, looking very wary. Luke said evenly, ''Let's spend the night together. Here. Then in the morning I'll drive back to the airport and we'll go our separate ways.''

Her lashes flickered. ''And what will that accomplish?''

''There's something going on between us, we both know that. This way we can have the best of two worlds…find out what it is without any messy complications.''

''Without any emotions, is that what you mean?''

''Without us getting entangled in a relationship neither of us wants!''

''You have it all figured out.''

''You can say no, Katrin,'' he said in a hard voice.

She glared at him, tilting her chin. ''I'm not going to do that.''

"So is that a resounding yes?"

"You don't want a resounding anything!"

"At least I'm honest about it."

"There are times," Katrin said trenchantly, "when you make me extraordinarily angry."

"Yes or no," Luke said.

"Yes," she blurted.

The bravado died from her face. She looked appalled; she looked as though she might change her mind any moment. Luke pushed back his chair with a jarring scrape of wood on wood. "Don't look so frightened...it'll be fine. You'll see." He walked around the table, took her cold hands and chafed them within his warmer ones. "Where's your bedroom?"

"Down the hall."

He pulled her to her feet and led the way, still clasping her by the hand. If ever there was a time for him to keep a lid on his own needs, it was now. No matter that Katrin had said Donald wasn't unkind; Luke would be willing to swear in any court in the land that her husband had been an inconsiderate and ungenerous lover. After all, he'd seen photos of the man. So it was up to him, Luke, to undo any damage that had been done. He was used to subduing his needs; it wouldn't be a problem.

The bedroom faced the woods behind the house, and was painted a clear green with white trim; the old-fashioned double bed was also painted white, covered with a woven throw. Luke drew the curtains, left his shoes by the wicker chair and hauled his shirt over his head. Then, casually, he put a couple of foil packets on the side table and turned to face Katrin.

She looked like the china doll on her bookshelves, stiff, immovable and wide-eyed. He wanted to sweep her into his arms and cover her with kisses. Instead Luke rested his hands on her shoulders, kneading them lightly, and let his lips wander from her cheekbones to her mouth. With infinite gentleness he dropped the lightest of kisses along its soft curve. ''You taste nice,'' he murmured.

''I don't know what—''

''Hush,'' Luke said softly, kissing her again, gossamer kisses that made his blood race in his veins. ''Everything'll be fine…we have the whole night just for ourselves. And all I want to do is give you pleasure.''

''But—''

He closed her mouth with his, stringently reining in his own appetites. This was for Katrin, not for him. With deliberate eroticism he slid his lips down her throat, and felt her shiver in response. Very delicately he traced the arc of her brow and the sweep of bone beneath her eye, letting his fingers slide down her smooth cheek to her lips, so exquisitely warm. With a shock of intimacy he felt the tiny puff of her breathing against his skin; and wondered if he'd be able to maintain his self-control.

Take it slow, Luke. Take it slow.

Suddenly and wholeheartedly, taking him by surprise, Katrin capitulated. With lingering pleasure, she kissed his fingers; then she cupped his face in her hands, kissing him full on the mouth. Like wildfire, the tantalizing pressure of her lips streaked through his body. Her palms moved to his bare chest, stroking it, brushing his nipples, then wrapping themselves around the taut muscles of his shoulders. Her body curved to meet his. And all the while she was nibbling at his lips with a sensual gentleness that set Luke's heart pounding in his chest. ''There's no rush,'' he muttered, and kissed her more deeply, her heated response hardening his groin.

He couldn't afford to lose his restraint. With all the skill he possessed, Luke set about showing her that he wasn't Donald Staines. His tongue dancing with hers, he carefully pulled the pins from her hair, so that it slid in a pale cascade down her back. Burying his fingers in its shiny weight, he kissed her throat, the line of her jaw, then her mouth again, plunging to taste its sweetness.

Her hands were probing the hard planes of his back, sliding down his spine; the press of her breasts against his rib cage set his head spinning. He struggled to slow the pace, when every nerve in his body was longing to throw her on the bed, throw himself on top of her, and bury himself within her. Because she was Katrin. Because he wanted her as he'd never wanted a woman before.

Don't be ridiculous, he told himself sharply. She's just a woman.

Against his lips, Katrin murmured, "I've got too many clothes on."

It had been part of Luke's plan to undress her slowly and deliberately, every move part of his seduction. But he could feel her tugging impatiently at her sweater; when he reached for the hem, his fingers met the warm, silky skin above the waistband of her jeans, and he forgot his plan in the fierce need to see her naked. He pulled the sweater over her head, tossing it on the chair. Her bra was white lace, cupping the sweet curves of her breasts, her skin like cream in the soft light from the hallway.

He almost lost it. He said hoarsely, "You're so beautiful, you take my breath away."

She gave a sudden laugh of delight. "I do?"

He drew her hips to his. "Indisputable evidence," he said; and watched her lips curve in a smile in which shyness and pride were irresistibly mixed.

She was showing her feelings, he realized; and knew he wasn't going to do the same. He didn't operate that way. He kissed her again, determined to control the moves. To control himself as he always did.

She was fumbling with his belt. "Take me to bed,

Luke,'' she said impetuously. "I'm not nervous anymore, can't you tell?''

Her eyes were a brilliant, depthless blue; her hips were swivelling suggestively against his body, in a way that made a mockery of technique and restraint. Luke reached for the metal button on her jeans, and drew the zipper down. Insensibly her eyes darkened. The pulse at her throat was throbbing against her skin. As he pushed the denim fabric down her hips, she helped him, laughing softly as it caught in her delicate lacy underwear.

He loved her laughter.

Loved it? thought Luke. What the hell kind of statement was that? He didn't know the meaning of the word *love,* and had no intentions of investigating it. So Katrin had a pretty laugh. So what?

"Luke?'' she whispered.

Inwardly cursing himself for losing his focus, Luke eased the denim down her thighs, his fingers pausing to stroke their slender length. Awkwardly she stepped out of her jeans. "Your turn,'' she said breathlessly.

Standing very still, Luke watched as she fumbled with his zipper, her head bent; the light shone in her hair. Of its own accord, his hand caressed its silken sheen. Like moonlight on water, he thought; and stopped himself from saying the words out loud. He'd never thought of himself as being at all poetic. What was happening to him? Then his trousers dropped to the floor. For a moment outside of control, Luke pulled Katrin against the length of his body, feeling the warm swell of her hips, the concavity of her spine, the push of her breasts to his torso as though he'd never been with a woman before. As though words like *hunger* and *need* were newly coined for this woman and this coupling.

Stow it, he thought dimly, and kissed her again. Then he reached around to undo the clasp of her bra; it joined his trousers on the floor. Like a man in a dream, he cupped her breasts in his palms, their soft weight arousing in him a possessiveness he could no more have stifled than he could have walked out of Katrin's bedroom. He bent his head, his mouth exploring her breasts' firm slopes, then the tautness of their rose-pink tips.

She was trembling very lightly. He said urgently, "Are you all right?"

Her laugh was shaky. "Oh Luke," she said artlessly, "I've never in my life felt so—so shameless."

Her words went straight through his defenses. She was saying she trusted him, he thought blankly. Trusted him enough to free her sexuality.

He mustn't misuse that trust. But equally he mustn't allow it to develop into anything else. With sudden impatience he stripped off his shorts, saying huskily, "Let's go to bed, Katrin."

Her movements imbued with a seductive grace, she pulled off the last of her garments, and again he was aware of the shyness lurking very close to her outer poise. He lifted her and laid her on the bed, her hair fanned on the pillows like a sweep of pale satin. For a moment he hovered over her, resting on his elbows, drinking in her beauty. Her courage, he thought. Her utter vulnerability. And with a clench at his heart knew he mustn't misuse these in any way, either.

He kissed her again, slowly lowering his body to hers, rubbing the roughness of his body hair to her sweet curves, always careful to keep his weight from crushing her. Before he was ready, she pulled him down hard on top of her, wrapping her thighs around his, murmuring his name in between fierce little kisses.

Cool it, Luke, cool it. Where's your famous technique?

Stroking her breasts, he lowered his head to lave her nipples with his tongue, hearing her moan with pleasure. Gradually he moved lower down her body, exploring with his hands and his mouth, discovering all her sensitivities. As he cupped the warm mound between her thighs, caressing the petals of her flesh with exquisite control, she cried out, begging him for more.

Only then did Luke take the little foil packet, deal with its contents, and slide into her. Her slick heat enveloped him; they fit as though they were made for each other. Now, he thought. Now. And knew as he watched the storm gather in her face that his timing was perfect. Her inner throbbing caught and magnified his own; he felt himself falling deeper and deeper into the cataclysm, joining her there.

But even then, Luke stifled the raw cry that was crowding his throat.

Resting some of his weight on his elbows, he dropped his head to her shoulder. His heartbeat eventually slowed, his breathing returning to normal. Gently he eased her onto her side and laid down facing her. She was lying still, her eyes closed. "Katrin?" he whispered. "Are you okay?"

She burrowed her face into his chest, as though not yet ready to look at him. "I'm fine," she mumbled, her breath warm on his chest. "What about you?"

"Great," he said.

She suddenly reared her head. "Really? Because you were holding back the whole time. You never really let go, even at the end."

He should have remembered how acute she was. "I wanted to make sure you were all right," he said; and knew it for only a partial reply.

"You didn't want to lose control."

"I hate postmortems," he said curtly.

"You hate it when I get too close to the truth. Too close to you."

For a man who only minutes ago had been convulsed by sexual passion, Luke felt extraordinarily angry. "So who did you prefer, Katrin? Me or Donald?"

"You. Of course. Donald was as self-centered in bed as out."

"I rest my case—I was trying to look after you, and I obviously succeeded."

"Why do I think I've been very cleverly sidetracked—and by a real pro?"

"You're putting the worst possible interpretation on everything I say and do!"

She pushed herself up on one arm. "So tell me about your parents, Luke. Your brothers and sisters and relatives. Where you grew up. Why you react so strongly to the mere mention of anything like a relationship."

"We made a deal. And that kind of talk's not in it."

"So we did," Katrin said. "In fact, I instigated it…silly me." With a brilliant smile that didn't quite reach her eyes, she added, "Since we've only got one night, we shouldn't waste any time…talk's certainly not getting us anywhere."

He was still angry. "For obvious reasons, I have to go to the bathroom."

"I hope you brought enough protection for the whole night," she said provocatively.

Luke stalked out of the room. But before he left the bathroom, he gazed at himself in the mirror. She hadn't liked him holding back; that was obvious. She saw it as a challenge. Well, she was out of luck. If she didn't like him as he was, too bad.

When he walked back in the room, she was lying just as he'd left her. He climbed into bed and lay down beside her. Her cheekbones were shadowed, as shadowed as her collarbone; darkness lay between her breasts. The dip of her waist, the rise of her hip, the smooth length of her thighs: all known to him now. And still desired, he realized with an unnerving jolt. Desired more strongly than before; the past three-quarters of an hour might never have happened.

She wasn't out of his system.

She'd become part of him instead. Invaded him in a way a woman never had before. Wouldn't that be closer to the truth?

The laugh was on him.

CHAPTER ELEVEN

As LUKE lay there, his mind racing, Katrin reached up, took his face between her palms and began kissing him with a slow sensuality that made his pulses quicken. Her fingertips light as feathers, she brushed his cheekbones, his deep-set eyes and the dark lines of his brows; as though she were blind and seeking an image of him in her mind. Then her lips wandered down the taut cords of his throat. And all the while, her body was pressed to his, moving against him with leisurely seductiveness.

He tried to hold back. Tried to take control. But as she teased his chest hair with one hand, her other hand slid lower. He was more than ready for her; and felt her touch surge through his body, flooding him with a primitive and all-consuming hunger. Her hair slipping like water over his ribs and navel, she moved lower, finding the jut of his hip-bones, his navel, the arrow of hair that led her mouth to the hardness that was need and the ache for consummation.

Luke shuddered with pleasure. She said softly, ''You're so silky, so warm,'' her tongue laving where her fingers had moved. He moaned deep in his throat, trapped by sensation. With the inexorability of fire, pleasure and hunger mounted, feeding on each other, hotter and hotter.

Just when he was sure he couldn't bear it any longer, Katrin slid away from him. She rolled on her back, thighs shamelessly spread, and took his hands in hers. ''Make love to me, Luke. As if this were the very first time for both of us... I want to know everything you can teach me.''

His heart pounding like a mallet in his chest, Luke said

with an honesty as naked as his body, "I've never wanted a woman as I want you."

She brought his hands to her breasts. "Touch me here…and here."

He plummeted to find her mouth, kissing her with an imperative hunger; then he licked the rise of her breasts, the hardness of her nipples, the long arc of each collarbone. Her hands were roaming his body, loosing in him waves of eroticism that he couldn't suppress and was helpless to resist.

As though the tides had engulfed him, Luke abandoned technique and control and restraint. Instead his own body and Katrin's ardent responses became his only guides in a territory new to him, that he'd never entered before. In a tumult of longing he caught her in his arms, kissing her, his fingers buried in her hair. She met him more than half-way, her generosity inflaming all his senses. Her taste, the delicate scent of her skin, the silken ripples of her hair, how would he ever get enough of them?

Drowning in passion, Luke sought to imprint himself on every inch of her body. Making it his; because she belonged to him. Impetuously he lifted her to straddle him, watching all the changing expressions on her face, so open and un-guarded. So alive. So utterly beautiful.

With a seductiveness that nearly drove him out of his mind, Katrin rode him slowly, her knees clasping his hips. When he touched her gently between her thighs, finding that place where she was most sensitive, she threw her head back, her breasts lifted, crying out his name over and over again. He could feel her inner pulsing as though it were his own, a release that triggered his. He rose to meet her, their gazes locked in an intimacy beyond anything he'd ever known. With a deep cry of satiation, he met her climax, and heard that cry echo in his ears.

With a long moan Katrin collapsed on top of him, her hair falling over his face like a shield that would shelter him from the world of normality. Her heart was racing against his chest; she felt boneless, so close to him that Luke wasn't sure where he ended and she began. He wound his arms around her and held on as though all his boundaries had dissolved. As though his very life depended on her.

He said nothing. There was nothing to say.

She slipped her knees farther down the bed, resting her cheek on his shoulder. Her arms were loosely curved to fit his body, her thighs enclosing his. Gradually he became aware that her breathing had slowed and deepened into sleep.

He lay still, eyes wide-open, one hand absently stroking her hair; in the turmoil of emotion that had him in its grip, a sense of rightness was predominant.

She belonged to him.

The words repeated themselves in his head. *Katrin belongs to me.* What was he thinking of? They were a lie, of course. Katrin didn't belong to him. She didn't want to. So how could he account for this deep current of possessiveness, the need to imprint himself on her so that she'd never go elsewhere?

Atavism, he told himself forcibly. The caveman asserting himself over all the constraints of a so-called civilized man. That's all it was.

He'd lost control. Totally. She'd seen to that.

Briefly he closed his eyes, suffused by a longing to simply go to sleep. To wake in her arms and make love again. To spend the day reading in her sunlit kitchen, waiting for her to come home from work; and then to go to bed with her once more. If his world had shifted in the last couple of hours, what would happen in two days? Two weeks?

Very carefully Luke shifted Katrin's sleeping body back onto the mattress. She stirred, her lashes fluttering; then she slipped back into sleep, her cheek buried in the pillow. His heart clenched. Defenseless, passionate, generous, fiery-tempered: what other facets of her personality had he not yet plumbed?

Would never plumb.

Because he was leaving. Now. He wasn't going to risk another of those cataclysmic matings.

He got out of bed with infinite care not to disturb her; and it was then that he saw the second foil packet on the table. He'd forgotten all about it; he'd never done that before.

She could be pregnant.

He wasn't going to follow that thought; the mere possibility was too overwhelming. All his movements clumsy, Luke got dressed in the semidarkness. Without a backward look he left the room, went down the hall and out to the kitchen. The side door creaked as he pulled it open. He froze, waiting for Katrin to call his name, wondering what he'd say if she did. But the house was encased in silence. He stepped outside, snipped the latch, got in his car and backed out of the driveway.

Because he lived in a city, he'd forgotten how completely dark the countryside could be. The vast panoply of stars was starkly lonely; it was a relief to see the lights of the resort through the trees. At the desk, not caring what the clerk thought, he checked out. Then he went upstairs, packed in a matter of minutes and left the room. Five minutes later, on the road that would eventually take him to the airport, Luke drove past Katrin's house in the village. But he saw no lights. No signs of life.

No indication that his own life had turned upside down in that little house on the shore of a vast lake.

He was running away. No question of it.

* * *

Two weeks later Luke and Ramon were seated in an oyster bar on Fisherman's Wharf. Through the open window they could see the crowded boardwalk, filled with tourists in bright clothes, with jugglers and musicians; and beyond them, the colorful prows of fishing boats. Everyone was having a good time, Luke thought sourly. Except for him.

Ramon raised his glass of beer. "Cheers, *amigo*. I'm glad you were free at such short notice." As they clinked glasses, he added, "Although you look like a man on death row."

"Thanks a lot," Luke said. When they'd played their regular tennis game last week, he'd been ignominiously defeated. He was sleeping lousily, Katrin haunted his thoughts night and day, and he bitterly regretted his impulsive trip to the resort. Other than that, he was fine.

Ramon said, "I have news for you. About the Staines murder case."

Luke plunked his glass down so hard that beer sloshed onto the table. "News?" he rapped.

"So you are still interested…I thought you might be."

"Give, Ramon."

"We've had a confession. And the DNA matches up. The case is solved, Luke. I know Katrin Staines was legally cleared at the trial…but a lot of people still thought she had something to do with it. Now we can prove she was completely innocent."

Luke sat back in his chair. The mellow strains of a jazz trumpet floated into the restaurant; a breeze ruffled the striped awnings. He pushed his dark glasses further up his forehead. "You're sure? About the confession, I mean?"

"It'll be in all the papers tomorrow morning. I wanted you to hear it from me first."

Luke said awkwardly, "You're a good friend."

"But not so good that you'll tell me what hold this Katrin has over you."

"If I ever figure it out, you'll be the first to know," Luke said with suppressed violence.

"I won't hold my breath," Ramon remarked. "The man who confessed, Edmond Langille, was a business associate of Donald's, who'd had a meeting with Donald earlier on the evening of the murder. Not one of the servants, of course, had seen him enter the house…where are witnesses when you need them? Nor did they see him leave, because he didn't. He overheard the row between Katrin and Donald and took full advantage of it instead."

"So why's he confessing now?"

"He's dying," Ramon said bluntly. "Cancer. Wants his conscience clear before he meets his Maker." Appreciatively Ramon chewed on his garlic bread, then forked a broiled oyster. "Katrin knew Edmond, although not well. So she'll have to come here for questioning."

"Not another trial?" Luke said, horrified.

"No, no. A formality, merely. I'll be phoning her this afternoon to make the arrangements."

Ramon then engrossed himself in his oysters, letting the silence hang. Luke said rapidly, "I went to Manitoba after you told me about her. We made love on the understanding we'd never see each other again."

Ramon said with an indifference that grated on Luke's nerves, "San Francisco's a big city. You don't have to see her… I can't imagine she'll stay long."

"I like my life the way it is!" Luke said violently.

"Then you are a fortunate man," Ramon said with a faint smile. "Eat your oysters before they get cold."

Paying very little attention to an excellent lunch, Luke cleared his plate, talking nonstop about the Democratic convention, the latest African coup and the price of gold. But as he and Ramon parted company on the boardwalk, Ramon said calmly, "Rosita would kill me for interfering—but Katrin's an exceptional woman, Luke. She could be the making of you. If you let her." He grinned. "See you at the courts next Tuesday. Try and have your mind on the game, *sí?*"

He walked away before Luke could reply, a big man easy in his own skin. Luke watched him go.

Katrin would be here in San Francisco. Soon. He'd have to phone her this evening.

He had to. He had no choice.

Luke phoned Katrin at ten-thirty her time. The phone rang six times; he was about to disconnect when she picked up the receiver. "Hello?" she said warily.

"Katrin, it's Luke." Now what was he supposed to say? *How are you?* "I hear you'll be coming to San Francisco."

"How did you know that?" she demanded.

"The police chief who's in command of the case is a good friend of mine. Ramon Torres."

"Just my luck that he'd be your friend."

"Ramon's a good man!"

"I couldn't agree more—even though he's a policeman, he was the one bright spot in the whole investigation," she said without a trace of emotion in her voice.

Silence hummed along the line. Wishing he could see her face, Luke said, "Are you there? Katrin?"

"I can't bear the thought of it all opening up again," she said raggedly. "I just can't bear it."

"But this will totally clear your name."

"I don't care anymore!"

He gripped the receiver tighter. "Are you crying?"

"No! I never cry…well, hardly ever."

"I want you to stay with me," he said.

"I've booked a hotel room."

"The media are going to be out in full force," Luke said, ruthlessly using the only weapon he could think of. "At my place you'll be protected from all that."

"It was over two years ago," Katrin cried, "what possible interest could they have in me now?"

"You're young, blond and beautiful. And you inherited a fortune."

"I gave it all away," she announced with defiant emphasis.

More than once he'd wondered why a rich woman like Katrin would be working as a waitress. Now he knew. He felt laughter rise in his chest. "Who to?"

"Shelters for the homeless. Soup kitchens. Overseas aid. You name it."

"No wonder the media are after you," Luke said. "That's not exactly standard behavior when someone inherits a whole wad of money."

"What was I supposed to do? Stay in a house I loathed, living off the shady dealings of a man I didn't love or respect? I don't think so."

Katrin would never be after his money, thought Luke. Not that he'd ever really thought she would be. "Have you booked your flight? I'll meet you at the airport and we'll go straight to my place."

"Luke," she said in a clipped voice, "I will not sleep with you."

"I haven't asked you to. Give me your flight times."

She made an indecipherable noise expressive of frustration and fury. Then he heard her shuffling papers. She read the information tonelessly, finishing, "I'll see you tomorrow. If you're not at the airport, I'll assume you've changed your mind."

"I won't change my mind. Goodbye, Katrin." Very quietly Luke replaced the receiver.

She didn't want to share his bed; she was sticking to the deal they'd made in the kitchen of her house. One night together and no more. All he had to do was stick to it, too.

And why wouldn't he? Hadn't he run away from all the implications of that passionate lovemaking in her little house beside the lake?

CHAPTER TWELVE

AT THE airport, Luke saw Katrin before she saw him. She was among the many deplaning passengers, searching for him in the crowd at the arrivals area. She was wearing a tailored lime-green suit, the jacket hip-length, fastened all the way to her throat with big gold buttons; the skirt was narrow-fitting, skimming her knees. Her hair was loose, straight, smooth and shiny. On her head she'd perched a lime-green straw hat, tilted at an audacious angle. She looked both sophisticated and unapproachable.

Not like the naked woman who'd twined herself around him just two weeks ago.

As Luke moved forward, Katrin caught sight of him. Briefly she faltered. But the other passengers carried her with them; seconds later, she was standing in front of him. Luke kissed her lightly on both cheeks. "You look very elegant."

"I'm a wreck."

"Then you're doing a wonderful job of hiding it. Let's get your luggage."

Her eyes kept flicking over the crowds; she was fiddling with the strap of her shoulder bag. Normally she wasn't a restless woman. As Luke took her by the arm, he discovered her muscles were as unyielding as a chunk of wood. He led the way to the carousel, where her one suitcase soon arrived. He picked it up. "I'm in the parking lot...let's go."

But as they emerged onto the sidewalk and the heat of a California afternoon, a crowd of reporters who had been waiting outdoors rushed toward them, mobbing them. A camera was thrust in Katrin's face, the bulb flashing with blinding rapidity. A barrage of questions was flung at her, microphones assaulting her on all sides. "Mrs. Staines, how does it feel to be back in San Francisco? What do you think about this latest development in the murder case? Did you ever suspect Edmond Langille was the murderer? Sir, your name, please?"

Luke said curtly, "Hang on, Katrin." Using her suitcase to shield her, his other arm tight around her shoulders, he pushed through the crowd with brute strength. But his strong-arm tactics only prolonged the interrogation; the reporters pursued them into the parking lot, their ceaseless questions shredding his self-control. "Is this man your lover, Mrs. Staines? Will you remarry now that you're proved innocent? Would you ever move back to San Francisco?"

His car was in one of the first rows. Luke dropped Katrin's case, unlocked the passenger door and pushed her down onto the seat, slamming the door in one man's face. He dumped her case in the trunk and went around to his side of the car. But before he got in, he said furiously, "What Mrs. Staines does with her life is none of your goddamned business—why don't you just leave her alone? You're a flock of vultures, and yes, you can quote me on that."

A flashbulb popped in his face. Ignoring it, he got in the car, put it in reverse, and accelerated backward. To his considerable satisfaction the reporters scattered like startled hens. He said tightly, "My God, I'm naive... I was expecting a couple of local journalists, but nothing like that. I don't know how they tracked you down. It sure wasn't anything I said."

He swung out of the lot, his anger still very close to the

surface. Aware that Katrin had yet to say a word, he glanced over at her. Her head was bent, her hands clenched in her lap. Even as he watched, a tear plopped onto the back of her left hand.

Swiftly Luke checked his rearview mirror to make sure none of the reporters was pursuing them. Then he pulled over into a business complex grouped with palm trees, and parked in the shade. "Katrin," he said urgently, "don't cry. They're not worth it."

Her knuckles tightened until the skin was white. Another tear splashed on her hand. As Luke put his arm around her and pulled her to his chest, her hat fell to the floor. He cradled her head to his shoulder, wishing with all his heart that he could protect her from the next couple of days.

But he couldn't.

He didn't like feeling so helpless. So inept.

Despite the heat, she was shivering; her tears soaked through his cotton shirt. He stroked her hair, murmuring her name, trying his best to comfort her. Then he heard her mutter, "I have to blow my nose."

He reached into the back of his car, grabbed the box of tissues and pulled out several, passing them to her. She blew her nose and wiped her tearstained cheeks. Her makeup was no longer impeccable; the tip of her nose was pink. Filled with a ridiculous tenderness, Luke said roughly, "I should have driven over the whole crew of them. Cameras and all."

With a shaky laugh, she said, "You'd have been put on trial for murder. It's not worth it, trust me."

That she could joke when she was so clearly upset brought on another of those irrational surges of tenderness. "I couldn't even protect you from them," Luke said in frustration.

Katrin looked right at him. "You did your best, and a

very impressive display it was. But the odds were something like twenty-five to one, Luke—give yourself a break.''

''Yeah…'' Very gently he reached over and dabbed at a tear on her jawline. ''You never cry. So you said.''

''Those reporters brought it all back,'' she said unevenly. ''On and on it went, day after day, until I thought I'd have hysterics, or else collapse in a puddle on the floor… I never did cry in front of them, though.''

''It's okay to cry in front of me,'' Luke said clumsily.

She shot him an unreadable glance, sat up straighter and said with attempted lightness, ''Fancy car.''

He'd said something wrong, although he had no idea what. But two could play that game. As he turned back on the road, Luke said, ''I always wanted a silver sportscar that could go from zero to sixty in less than five seconds. Is your hat okay?''

She bent to pick it up, then rolled the window partway down, leaned back in her seat and closed her eyes. She murmured, ''Wake me when we get there.''

Luke took the 101 and gunned the engine. He needed a respite; there'd been altogether too much emotion in the last half hour. But before he was quite ready for it, he was turning into his driveway in Pacific Heights. Katrin stirred, opening her eyes. ''This is your house?''

He nodded. ''The owner before me didn't like Georgian brick. So he tore down the original house and built this instead.''

''Minimalist,'' she said politely.

''Hideous,'' said Luke.

''Deconstruction's all the rage.''

''Tear it down, you mean?'' He laughed, delighting in her mischievous smile. ''I'm about ready to sell it and move outside the city. Or maybe to Presidio Heights, I've seen a couple of places I like there. Let's go in.''

After he'd unlocked the front door, Katrin entered ahead of him, preceding him into the living room with its sparse, modern furniture. "The view is wonderful," she said spontaneously.

He could see all the way from the Golden Gate Bridge to Fisherman's Wharf; the island of Alcatraz loomed above the cold, choppy waters of the bay, where sailboats bobbed like white-painted toys. "Can I get you a drink?"

"I need to clean up," she said.

He took her past the dining room and the library up a short flight of stairs to the guest wing. Her bedroom also had a wide view of the bay, and came with its own balcony. "My room's upstairs," he said briefly. "You'll be entirely private here."

She slid her feet out of her Italian pumps. "I might have a nap," she said evasively, "I didn't sleep well last night, and I'll need my wits about me tomorrow. Will you call me whenever you want dinner?"

"I went to the deli, got a bunch of stuff we can reheat in the microwave." His smile felt stiff. "I'm no cook."

"That'll be fine... I just need to be alone for a while."

Her body language was easily read: keep your distance. Luke nodded coolly, closed her door and walked back to the living room. He was the one who'd run away from her so he wouldn't make love to her again; but right now he'd have given his eyeteeth to have been in bed with her.

Go figure.

Cursing himself under his breath, he changed into shorts and a tank top in his room and spent an hour in the fully equipped gym on the upper floor. Then he heard Katrin moving around downstairs. He ran down in his bare feet;

she'd changed into white cotton pants and a pink shirt. "Ready to eat?" he asked.

Her lashes flickered. "Whenever you are."

"You don't have to be so polite!"

"How else are we supposed to deal with this?"

"We slept together, Katrin—or are you forgetting that?"

"I slept. You left."

He flinched. "Okay, okay...come on through to the kitchen."

"I wish you'd put some clothes on first," she said irritably.

"I'm wearing clothes."

In a deadly quiet voice she said, "Why did you leave in the middle of the night, Luke?"

"Why did you say on the phone that we wouldn't make love again?"

"I don't see why I have to answer that."

"Fine. That can work both ways."

She glared at him. "I have yet to see a single photo in this house. Or anything personal. It's like a house in a magazine, perfect and soulless. Don't you have any photos of your parents?"

"Obviously not," he said shortly, and went on the attack. "Are you pregnant, Katrin? We didn't use anything that second time."

"No. I'm not."

His chest tight with a mixture of emotions he couldn't possibly have sorted out, although relief and a sharp regret were certainly among them, Luke marched into the kitchen. Which did indeed look perfect and soulless. "Let's eat... I thought we'd go out on the balcony."

He reached into the refrigerator. "The salads can go on plates from the cupboard over the sink. I'll heat up the chicken and the garlic bread."

The kitchen was large. But as he took out a platter for the chicken, he bumped into Katrin as she turned to ask him something. The platter landed on the counter. He put his arms around her and kissed her with a blatant and smoldering sensuality that, after the briefest of hesitations, she more than matched. His body on fire with need, he found her breast under her pink shirt, its warmth and weight so well remembered, so greatly desired.

She yanked her head free and struck at his hand. "Don't, Luke! We can't do this."

"Why not? We both want to," he said with infallible logic.

"We agreed we wouldn't."

"Agreements can be renegotiated."

"I can't take this anymore," she said incoherently, "it's all too much!"

Remembering with compunction the reason she was here, Luke said slowly, "You're right on the edge, aren't you?"

"You got that right. Don't you see? I made the biggest mistake of my life when I married Donald. Who was a very rich man. And now here I am back in the same city involved with another rich man."

"I don't do shady deals," Luke grated. "And I'm not asking you to marry me."

"How true...you're not, are you?" she said in a peculiar voice. "I'll be here three days...so are you suggesting we have three successive one-night stands? Is that it?"

"That sounds so damn crude!"

"I call it like I see it."

Her cheeks were now as pink as her shirt; but there was real desperation in her blue eyes. Luke said carefully, "Look, you've got a heavy-duty day ahead of you tomorrow, Katrin. Why don't we call a truce? At least until you're done with the police and the fancy lawyers.''

"And then we'll pick up where we left off?" she snorted.

"Why not?" He grinned at her. "It was a very nice kiss."

"I could think of several words to describe that kiss. Nice isn't one of them.''

"Oh? Do tell."

Hands on her hips, she glowered at him. "You're one heck of an infuriating man, Luke MacRae...do you have a middle name, by the way?"

"Where I come from, they didn't go in for middle names," Luke muttered; then could have bitten off his tongue.

"And if I were to ask you where that was, you'd shut up tighter than the proverbial clam."

He raked his fingers through his sweat-damp hair. "Supper. On the balcony. Isn't that what we came out here for?"

She grabbed a white dish towel from the rack, waving it in front of him. "And the truce—don't forget the truce."

He suddenly started to laugh. "You won't let me."

Her lips curved in an answering smile. "You're getting the picture. What kind of chicken did you buy?"

Fifteen minutes later they were seated on teak chairs amidst the tangle of vines and flowering shrubs on the balcony; the bay and the distant hills were topped by a pearl-gray evening sky. Luke filled Katrin's wineglass with a California Chardonnay. "To better days," he said.

"I'll drink to that." She tore off a chunk of hot garlic bread, licked her fingers and said with a sigh, "I feel much better. Let's talk about movies and Paris and whether you're afraid of snakes."

"It's spiders that do me in," he said solemnly, and obligingly asked her what movies she'd seen lately, buried as she was in Askja. One thing led to another, until Luke found himself telling her stories about some of his jaunts into mines ranging from the Arctic to the tropics. Her questions were intelligent, her interest genuine: encouraged, he talked far longer than was his custom, revealing more of himself than he'd intended. Peeling her a ripe peach, he said, "You're a good listener."

"I've learned more about you in the last hour than since we met." She licked peach juice from her fingers. "With the exception of when we were in bed."

His knife skidded dangerously close to the ball of his thumb. "And what did you learn about me there?"

"How closely you guard yourself and your secrets," Katrin said. "How passionate you can be, when you allow those barriers to drop."

"Did I have a choice?" Luke heard himself ask; then added in true fury, "I thought we'd set up a truce."

"Why did you leave in the middle of the night?" she said for the second time, a dangerous glint in her eye.

"You're as bad as those reporters!"

"No, I'm not—because I care about the answer," she retorted. "Don't you see? You give me a glimpse of the real man, and then you run like crazy in the opposite direction...why, Luke?"

He pushed back his chair, his shoulders rigid. "I'm going to put some coffee on...can I get you more wine?"

"You're doing it again!"

"You have a choice here, Katrin," he said, each word dropping like a stone. "Take me as I am. Or back off."

"That's not a choice. It's an ultimatum. And you know it."

"It's all you're being offered."

"No coffee. No wine," she said, her eyes almost black

in the dusk. "I'm going to bed. I'll see you in the morning."

But as she marched around a tall potted cactus, Luke took her by the waist, pulled her toward him and kissed her with an explosive mixture of desire and fury. Before she could respond, he pushed her away. "Sleep well," he said. "I'll drive you to the police station in the morning."

"No, you won't—I'll get a cab."

"You will not."

"I hate domineering men!"

"I'm just being a good host," he said smoothly. "Good night, Katrin."

She whirled, slid open the glass doors and vanished inside the house. Luke drained his wineglass, gazing out over the brilliant lights of the city and the slick, dark waters of the bay. Whether he went to bed with Katrin or not, he was getting in deeper merely by being within ten feet of her.

Why had he invited her here? This house, even though he no longer liked it, was still his sanctuary, where he could drop his public persona and simply be himself. Be as private as he liked. Why hadn't he listened to Ramon? *San Francisco's a big city,* the burly policeman had said...*you don't have to see her.*

The mood he was in, the reporters had better keep their distance tomorrow.

When Luke picked Katrin up at the front entrance of the police station late the following afternoon, the reporters were clustered around the side door. She got in quickly, and Luke drove away. She was wearing her lime-green suit without the hat, her hair in a loose knot. She said faintly, "Ramon let the word slip I'd be going out the side door. And they fell for it."

Luke eased into the flow of traffic. "How did it go?"

"I'm finished. I can go home."

His palms were suddenly cold on the wheel. He wasn't ready for her to leave. Not yet. "There's a big charity ball tonight at one of the hotels on Nob Hill, I've had the tickets for a couple of weeks. I think we should go."

She sat up straight. "Are you out of your mind? The last thing I want to do is go out in public."

"Ashamed of me, Katrin?"

"Don't be obtuse! After the spread in today's papers, you think I should go to a function full of people I met years ago, with a man the media are insinuating is my lover?"

The newspapers had certainly gone to town; the photo of his furious face as he'd tried to shield a beautiful woman in a wide-brimmed hat had made the front pages. No one at his office had mentioned it, they'd known better; but all day there'd been a tendency for silence to fall as soon as he entered a room. Luke said forcibly, "You've done nothing wrong, nothing to be ashamed of. Why should you leave here under a cloud? Blazon it out, that's the only way to go."

"You're nuts."

"We're going to Union Square to buy you an evening gown. You can fly home tomorrow."

"You're also autocratic, overbearing and tyrannical!"

"I'm a very good dancer as well," he said, stopping for a red light and smiling at her. "Do you like to dance?"

She scowled at him. "I love to. Add conceited."

"We can trade insults while the band's taking its breaks."

"Have I just been coerced into doing something that I know I shouldn't?"

He swung around a corner, then sneaked another glance at her. "Yep."

Her eyes narrowed. "What's in this for you, Luke? A new twist? Something to relieve the tedium of your life?"

He said flatly, "I can't answer that. Because I don't know what to say."

"Well, that's honest at least."

"Do we have to analyze everything we do?"

"If I'm analyzing, it's called self-protection," Katrin said vigorously. "I'm not sure you're aware of the effect you have just by entering a room. Every woman between puberty and senility stares at you as if you're the best thing since sliced bread. Regrettably, I have to include myself among them."

Heat crept up his neck. "Shove it, Katrin."

"I'm telling the truth! You're the sexiest man I've ever laid eyes on."

Wishing he could gun the car, but forced to crawl at five miles an hour because of the traffic, Luke muttered, "You're exaggerating and you know it."

"I am not. Anyway, to get back to this charity ball—I can't afford an evening gown. I'm saving to go to law school."

"It's a present. From me." He took a deep breath, quelled the panic in his gut, and added, "To say I'm sorry I left in the middle of the night."

To his dismay the light at the next intersection turned orange. He pulled up behind an SUV. Katrin said quietly, "For the third time, Luke, why did you leave?"

"Because I was afraid to stay."

"*Afraid?*"

"That's what I said." For Pete's sake, he thought, fuming, why couldn't the light change?

"Afraid of me?"

"Afraid of what you do to me," he said shortly.

In a small voice she said, "I thought you didn't like making love to me, and that's why you left."

His jaw dropped. "Didn't *like* it? Are you serious?"

The driver behind him blasted on the horn. The light was green; Luke pressed hard on the accelerator. Katrin said crossly, "What else was I supposed to think? I figured I was—despite my marriage, or perhaps because of it—too inexperienced for you. Too gauche. Too unsophisticated."

She couldn't have been further from the truth. "I ran away because I hate losing control," he said harshly.

Her fingers slowly relaxed in her lap. "So I've noticed."

"You notice too much," Luke announced. "I don't know what it is about you, but I've told you more in the last month than I've ever told Ramon, whom I've known for years."

"It's my big blue eyes," she said pertly.

He pulled into a parking garage north of the square, his mouth set. "You're going to buy a gorgeous dress and anything else you need to go with it. Money is no object and don't argue."

"No, sir," she said in a perfect imitation of her waitressing voice.

Luke started to laugh, his ill humor dissolving. "I'm beginning to think I led a very boring life until you came along."

They left the car and walked south, the clang of cable car bells accompanying them. At the edge of the square with its palm trees, clipped hedges and massed flowerbeds, Luke asked, "Want to start at Saks?"

Her cheeks pink, Katrin said, "I don't want you to see the dress until this evening."

He grinned at her. "In that case I'll find a bar, and you can come and get me when you're ready."

He had time to slowly drink a glass of Chablis and read

the entire newspaper before Katrin reappeared. She said breathlessly, "I've run up rather large bills at three different stores."

"Good," said Luke; and half an hour later, several boxes in the trunk of the car, was driving toward Pacific Heights. They had a snack in the kitchen to tide them over until the dinner at the hotel, then Katrin disappeared to get dressed. Luke went upstairs, showered and shaved, and got into his tuxedo. He didn't have a clue what was going on, although he was quite sure if he had any sense he wouldn't be taking Katrin to a charity ball where he'd meet just about everyone he knew; and discovered that he didn't care.

He felt alive. Disturbingly and wholeheartedly alive.

Which implied, of course, that he'd been going through the motions for a very long time.

CHAPTER THIRTEEN

LUKE was waiting in the living room when he heard Katrin on the stairs of the guest wing. He walked through to the hallway; and when he saw her, stopped dead. Her dress, sleeveless and form-fitting, was made of black fishnet adorned with intricate patterns of multicolored feathers: it was an outrageous dress, that she wore with panache. Her sandals were stiletto-heeled, her makeup dramatic, her hair a smooth sweep of gold. He said in a cracked voice, "Katrin…"

She stopped two steps above him. "Do you like it?"

"You look magnificent."

She blushed. "It's the dress. Very expensive."

"It's the woman wearing the dress," he said. "You also look very sexy."

Her flush deepened. "I could say the same of you."

"A penguin compared to a bird of paradise?"

Her laughter, as always, entranced him. "Actually," she said, "they're dyed rooster feathers, I checked just in case they'd used endangered birds." She descended the last two steps. "And I don't feel at all sexy. I feel, if you want the truth, extremely nervous."

"You don't need to be nervous," Luke said. He held out his arm; his voice roughened. "I'm with you every step of the way, and I'll look after you to the best of my ability."

Had he ever felt such a tumult of raw sexual longing and possessiveness? But that wasn't all that was new. His instinctive need to protect her, to support her in any way he could, was something he'd never experienced with any other woman. As she tucked her arm in his, he rested the fingers of his free hand on hers, their warmth searing him with desire.

She said unsteadily, "When you look at me like that, I melt."

"Like ice cream on a sunny day?" he said, his heart pounding under his pleated white shirt.

She glanced down at her pastiche of feathers. "Mint, cherry and blueberry mist."

"If I kiss you," Luke said deliberately, "I'll get scarlet lipstick all over me."

"You could kiss my cheek."

Instead, his face intent, Luke leaned over and slid his mouth down her throat, her delicate perfume tantalizing his nostrils. She quivered in response, her blue eyes brilliant as jewels. "We'll be late for dinner," she whispered.

He stepped back, his gaze trained on her vividly expressive features. "That was the aperitif."

"I can hardly wait for the main course."

What did she mean—that when they got home tonight, she wanted to make love to him? "Not to mention dessert," he said. Impulsively, he raised her hand to his lips, kissing her fingers with lingering pleasure. When he looked up, he could have sworn there were tears in her eyes. "Katrin?" he said in quick concern.

"It's nothing...so often you take me by surprise." Her smile as brilliant as her eyes, she added, "Let's go. We'll take them by storm."

Which, Luke thought midway through the evening, was exactly what they'd done. Friends and associates of his had made a point of introducing themselves to Katrin with genuine pleasure; while old friends of hers were clearly happy to see her again. The others, gossips and rivals, he didn't care about. Within half an hour of arriving in the elegant ballroom, Katrin had relaxed. Her poise, her dignity and friendliness, weren't new to him; but to see her in his own setting among his compatriots had a sense of rightness about it that both pleased and alarmed him.

He was getting in deeper with every passing minute; and couldn't, for the life of him, have pulled back. The signals between him and Katrin were unmistakable; he knew in his bones that the evening would end with her in his bed.

Where she belonged.

They were dancing a samba at two in the morning when she said, out of the blue, "Thank you, Luke."

Her hips were swaying, all her movements so graceful that he was on fire with wanting her. "For what?"

"For suggesting we do this." She gave him a sly grin. "Or should I say, for insisting we do this...and for taking such good care of me all evening."

He led her through some intricate footwork. "Not exactly difficult."

"I mean it," she said with sudden intensity.

He said huskily, "I think we should go home."

She looked at him through her lashes. "Because my feet hurt?"

"Because my tie's choking me."

"If you take off my shoes, I'll take off your tie."

"Best offer I've had all evening."

"I should hope so," said Katrin.

They left the ballroom amidst a chorus of goodbyes, and drove back to Pacific Heights in a silence charged with the unspoken knowledge of what they were about to do. Once in the house, Luke picked Katrin up in his arms, carried her upstairs to his room, and then, looking down at her, said, "In the movies, I'd fling you on the bed and rip the dress from your body. But, quite frankly, I don't have a clue how to get you out of all those feathers."

She chuckled. "If you put me down on the floor, I'm sure you can find the zipper that's very cleverly hidden among the black zigzags."

Instead Luke put her down on the edge of the bed, then knelt in front of her, removing her elegant sandals one by one. As she wriggled her toes in relief, he smoothed her arches in his hands, rubbing her heels and stroking her ankles with a slow, sensual pleasure. Then he felt her very lightly caressing his hair. As he glanced up, her beauty struck him anew, piercing him to the core. He said jaggedly, "I'm the luckiest man in San Francisco right now. Hell, in the whole wide world."

Her response was to lean forward and find his mouth with hers, kissing him until his whole body was nothing but raw need. With awkward haste they undressed each other, the feathered dress crumpling on the carpet in a froth of color. Then Katrin's naked body was beneath his, and Luke forgot everything but a craving to give her the most intense pleasure he was capable of. As she opened to him with an ardent generosity that touched him to the heart, he was freed of any constraint; they climaxed all too soon, their cries of satiation mingling in the darkness.

Luke lay still, his breathing harsh in his ears. He was, he realized, most passionately himself at the exact moment that he lost himself within her.

What did that mean?

He said unevenly, "Kind of a rush job."

"We have all night, Luke."

There was the faintest shadow of a question in her words. He said roughly, "All night. All week. All month...don't go back tomorrow, Katrin. Stay."

"All right," she said.

With an incredulous laugh, Luke said, "Just like that?"

"You like what we do together in bed—don't you?"

"Nah...I'm only putting up with it so I won't hurt your feelings." Then he reared up on his elbow, stroking her hair back from her forehead. "Give me five minutes and

I'll show you how much I like it. I can't get enough of you, Katrin, you're in my blood and my bones.''

"And you in mine," she said in a low voice. "Make love to me, Luke. As I've never been made love to before…''

"My pleasure," he said huskily, and set out to do just that.

The days and nights passed, one by one. During the days, Luke worked as hard as he'd ever worked; even though he whistled as he ran up the flights of stairs to his office, and smiled more at his staff, his focus was absolute, his efficiency unimpaired. At night, he made love to Katrin; and woke sometimes in the night to find her asleep beside him, her soft breathing so familiar, so much a part of him.

He kept these two compartments of his life completely separate. He didn't invite Katrin up to his office or to have lunch with any of his staff; he didn't bring work home from the office. This arrangement worked fine for him. Sex with Katrin—living with Katrin—might be a form of divine madness. But the rest of his life was totally under control. Just as it should be.

When they'd been together almost two weeks, he was driving up the street toward his house after work when he screeched to a halt. The front garden, attractively landscaped with cacti and ornamental grasses, had been taken over by a flock of large, supremely ugly, pink plastic flamingos. In the middle of them a large white sign said, Happy Birthday, Luke.

He stared at them, torn between laughter and something akin to panic. He never made a deal of his birthday. His father, as far as he could tell, had never really wanted him; certainly his mother hadn't. So why celebrate a day that was completely meaningless?

Somehow Katrin had found out that today was his birthday.

He didn't like her knowing even that smallest of secrets.

Luke parked in the driveway and walked up to the front door. Each flamingo sported a white satin bow around its neck, and had long black lashes painted over demurely downcast eyes. Where in heaven's name had she found anything so tacky?

He unlocked the front door. She came out of the kitchen, wearing loose cotton pants and an apple green shirt, her hair in a long braid down her back. "Happy birthday," she said jauntily.

"I hope you're only renting those ornithological disasters."

She pouted. "You don't like them?"

He grinned; how could he help it? "You're lowering the tone of the neighborhood."

"The neighborhood's too stuffy by far. Be glad I didn't choose purple pandas."

"I never told you when my birthday was."

"Your driver's licence fell out of your wallet one day. I saw the date when I picked it up. Come into the kitchen."

The kitchen ceiling was aquiver with helium balloons. A birthday cake, one side sagging slightly, was sitting on the counter; it bristled with candles. Katrin reached in the refrigerator, took out a bottle of Dom Pérignon, and expertly blew the cork. She poured two glasses, passing one to Luke. "To celebrate the fact that you were born," she said.

The bubbles prickled his nose. "Did you make the cake?"

"I did. I'm no pro when it comes to cakes. But first we're going out for dinner. My treat. The dress code's casual."

Half an hour later, Luke saw why. She took him to Chinatown; arm in arm, they strolled the busy streets, past tea houses, flashing neon signs, roofs shaped like pagodas, and tiny grocery stores crammed with Chinese vegetables. In the narrow alleys, wind chimes vied with the clatter of mah-jongg tiles, the air pungent with joss sticks. The restaurant Katrin had chosen was small and intimate; the pot stickers and Cantonese-style bass were the best Luke had ever eaten.

Afterward, they went home and had cake; then Katrin, without much difficulty, seduced him. As she drifted off to sleep in his arms, she murmured, "Did you enjoy your birthday?"

"I did," Luke said, and discovered to his surprise that this was true. "When do the flamingos fly south?"

"Tomorrow morning at nine o'clock."

"Good," he said, and in a surge of tenderness kissed her cheek. "Good night, darling Katrin," he whispered.

But she was asleep.

Early in the morning two days later, Katrin and Luke were sitting on the balcony drinking coffee and reading the papers. She passed him another slice of toast and said casually, "I'm coming downtown later on today, can I drop into your office to say hello? I'd like to see where you work."

Luke glanced up from the headlines. "I don't think that's such a good idea."

"No?"

Her blue eyes were looking straight at him. Refusing to back down, Luke said, "I like to keep business just that— business. Nothing to do with what goes on here, in the house. I've always kept the two separate, this is nothing to do with you personally."

She bit her lip. "Work is a big part of your life. It pays for everything we do. I'd like to know more about it."

"I've told you about some of my latest deals."

"I'd like to meet your staff. Joe and Lindy and the rest."

"No, Katrin," Luke said, restlessly shuffling the newspaper. "You met some of my friends at the charity ball, that's enough."

Small flags of temper stained her cheeks. "You told me once you've never been married. Have you ever been in love?"

"No."

"Have you ever wanted children?"

"No."

"Have you ever lived with someone? Other than me."

"No."

"What's so special about me, Luke?"

He could feel his own temper rising. "Do we have to dissect what's going on? Why can't we just let it be?"

"I'll tell you why. Because you're virtually a stranger to me. Sure, I know your body as I know my own, and you've freed my sexuality for the first time in my life. Both those things are hugely important and utterly wonderful. But other than that, you're an unknown quantity. There isn't a single personal photograph in this house, I know nothing about your past, where you come from, what made you the way you are. It's as though the past doesn't exist for you."

"It's irrelevant. What happens here and now is what's important."

"I want to know more about you!"

"Then you're out of luck."

"You know a great deal about me. I've talked to you about my parents, my disastrous marriage, the trial. Why can't you reciprocate?" She suddenly paled. "Did you do something terrible? Is that what it is?"

"Stop it, Katrin!" he exploded. "I'm not a criminal, if that's what you're implying."

"Then tell me!"

"You want all of me, don't you?" he said bitterly. "You can't be satisfied with what you've got."

"I want the whole man. Not just the lover."

He pushed back his chair, flinging the paper on the table. "I've got to go, or I'll be late for work."

She stood up too, her slim body in its silk robe limned by the early sun. "You're going to Dallas the day after tomorrow, on business. Take me with you... I can easily amuse myself in the daytime."

"It's only for four days. There's plenty here for you to amuse yourself with."

"But I want to be with you."

"No," he said in a hard voice, pulled the glass door open and ran upstairs to finish dressing. What was the matter with her? Their life together was perfect. Why did she have to go messing around with it? Spoiling it?

But by late afternoon, when it was time for him to head home, Luke was aware of an uneasy mixture of guilt and compunction. He hadn't changed his mind about Dallas. But he could have phrased his refusal rather more diplomatically. And wasn't the incredible physical closeness between him and Katrin far more significant than a disagreement about something as silly as a business trip? On impulse he stopped off at Union Square, choosing after some thought an Italian gold filigree bracelet and matching earrings. He had them boxed and wrapped, then drove home.

Katrin was in the kitchen. She was an erratic cook, rarely satisfied to leave a recipe as it was; tonight's shrimp salad, however, looked entirely successful. He said casually, "I bought you a present."

She put down the paring knife. Staring at the elegantly wrapped package in his hand, she said in a strained voice, "Please, Luke, will you take me to Dallas?"

"I already said no. Aren't you going to open this?"

"I don't want presents. I want you. All of you."

"I'm getting tired of saying no."

"Then try yes for a change."

"Yes, you're being unreasonable and demanding. Yes, you're ruining what we've got by hankering after more."

"Are you saying I'm greedy?" Katrin snapped.

"I'd be willing to bet that what we share upstairs in the bedroom is fifty times better than most couples on this block. But are you satisfied? No, you're not. If I give you the moon, you'll want the stars. If I give you the stars, you'll want the whole universe."

Her voice rose. "That's not true. Just because I want to know more about you doesn't make me into some kind of insatiable monster."

Luke tossed the box on the counter. "I really hate coming home from work and having a fight before I even have the chance to take my tie off."

"Would you rather I pretend everything's wonderful when it's not? When I'm unhappy?"

Unhappy. Hastily Luke buried this word deep in his psyche. "I'd rather you stopped being a romantic dreamer. This is real life, Katrin. Real life has limits and boundaries. I'm not some sort of hero you can shape to fit your own ends."

"Are all men alike?" she flashed. "Donald wanted a cipher for a wife. Someone who kept the house running smoothly, who could act as a hostess for his friends. Someone to warm his bed when he remembered to get into it. And like a fool, I fell for it. Don't get me wrong, Luke—in most ways you're totally different from Donald. But you want me to fit a certain mold, too. Be your mistress but not your wife. Share your body but not your soul." Her eyes were as adamant as sapphires. "You've got the wrong woman."

"I'm beginning to think I have," he said.

She drew in her breath sharply, as though he'd physically hit her. "I'm going for a walk," she muttered, grabbed the spare key from the ring by the door and ran from the kitchen.

Luke didn't run after her. Discovering he'd been gripping the edge of the counter so hard his fingertips were white, he made a huge effort to relax. He'd been so careful all his life to choose women who wanted nothing more of him than he was willing to give. But with Katrin, he'd blown it.

She wanted all of him.

There was no way she would get it.

Luke was just starting to worry when he heard Katrin unlock the front door. He came out of the den, where he'd been watching some mindless TV, more relieved to see her than he was going to admit to himself or her. Hadn't he been wondering if she'd taken the first flight north?

He said noncommittally, "Nice walk?"

She stopped several feet away from him. "Have you changed your mind? About Dallas, I mean?"

"You should know me better than that."

"Then I'll sleep in the guest room tonight."

"Using your body as a bargaining chip?"

"That's a cheap shot!"

"I'm not retracting it."

"I feel a million miles away from you," Katrin said with desperate intensity. "How can I share your bed?"

"Our bed."

"That's the only place that's really ours. Everything else is yours."

"So we're back to square one," Luke said harshly.

"I guess we are." Standing tall, she said, "Good night, Luke."

The words burst from him. "Katrin, don't do this!"

"I don't know what else to do. How else to handle it."

Before she could walk past him, he seized her by the

wrist; her sweater was damp from the fog that had swathed the city all day. With a distant part of his brain, he saw drops like dew on her hair, glittering as brilliantly as diamonds.

"Don't!" she cried, and tried to pull away.

As quickly as he'd grabbed her, Luke let go. As if he were four years old again, back in the old kitchen in Teal Lake, he remembered his father wrapping his fingers around his mother's wrist, then shoving her hard against the wall, pinning her there with his big body. He, Luke, shouldn't have been so critical of his mother because she'd left a violent, drunken man. What he still found hard to forgive was that she'd abandoned her small son; and had never once been in touch with him since.

"Luke, don't look like that," Katrin whispered. "What's wrong?"

He stepped back, wiping his hands down the sides of his trousers. "I'm not going to beg you to share my bed, we've gone too far for that," he said curtly. "Good night, Katrin."

She made the smallest of gestures toward him. But he turned away, going back into the den as though whatever was on TV was more important than she was. Through the canned laughter of a sitcom, he heard her footsteps retreat toward the guest wing, then the quiet closing of the adjoining door.

Luke flicked the power off, staring at the blank screen as if it could give him some answers.

CHAPTER FOURTEEN

LUKE got up very early the next morning and left the house almost immediately. He didn't want to see Katrin. He was as bereft of answers in the morning as he had been the night before; and just as angry.

He worked out at the gym adjoining the tennis court, showered, and had breakfast at a little diner he knew. Then he went to the office and threw himself into his newest project with a driven energy that had all his staff on tiptoes. After ordering a sandwich at his desk for lunch, he worked until nearly six. The last thing he did before leaving the office was to make sure all his arrangements for Dallas were in place. One passenger. Traveling alone.

Katrin was in the kitchen when Luke got home. As he leaned over to kiss her, she turned her head so that he kissed her cheek rather than her lips. He said evenly, "Want to go out for supper?"

"I made a meat loaf, except I tried marinated tofu instead of beef," she said in a staccato voice. "It tastes a bit weird."

"But very good for us."

She bit her lip. "Luke, I'll make a deal with you. I won't mention Dallas again if you'll promise me four days of your time when you get back. We'll go somewhere of my choice, and you won't ask any questions until we get there."

He put his briefcase on the counter. "You're still angry."

"Will you do it?"

"Playing games with me?"

147

"No more than you are with me."

He loosened his tie and dropped his jacket over a chair. "I don't think I am. And I don't like being manipulated."

"I don't like being excluded."

His voice hardened. "I'm not going to change, Katrin. Not for you or for anyone."

"Four days, Luke. That's all I'm asking."

Even as it infuriated him, he was reluctantly admiring her spirit. She had it all worked out. He was getting four days without her in Dallas. She'd get four days with him heaven knows where. But wasn't that better than the stalemate of the last twenty-four hours? He'd slept lousily last night, his bed a wasteland without her.

"I'll tell you one thing, living with you isn't dull," he said irritably. "I agree."

"Thank you," she said, and reached for the spice rack.

The jeweler's box, fully wrapped, was still lying on the counter. "Are you ever going to open that present?"

"The present I want, you're not prepared to give," she said edgily. "And money can't buy it. So what am I supposed to do—make do with substitutes?"

"You're the only woman I've known who'd turn down a Tiffany's box!"

"Adversity's good for the character," she retorted. "Or at least, that's what I keep telling myself. And sure, I'm curious to know what's in it—I'm only human."

"I didn't buy you something to make up for not taking you to Dallas," Luke said, his words falling over one another. "I bought it because waking up in the night and finding you there beside me makes me happier than I've ever been in my life."

Dammit, he'd done it again. Said more than he'd ever meant to say, just because a woman with big blue eyes was pushing him beyond his limits.

Those same blue eyes were now filmed with tears. "It does?" Katrin said jaggedly.

"Surely I don't have to tell you that?"

"It would be really nice if reading your mind was one of my talents," she said. "But it isn't."

Luke didn't want her reading his mind; he had to keep some parts of himself inviolate. "I didn't sleep more than five consecutive minutes last night."

"Neither did I." Giving him a small smile, Katrin reached for the jeweler's box. As she lifted the delicate bracelet from the box, her face lit with delight. "It's beautiful, Luke, thank you. Will you do it up for me?"

He fumbled with the tiny clasp, her scent filling his nostrils. When he kissed the pulse in her wrist, it raced beneath his lips; they were very late eating the marinated tofu. Which did indeed taste rather weird.

Luke went to Dallas on his own, missed Katrin unrelentingly, and flew home late on Friday. He didn't like missing her, reaching for her in the night, wanting to share a joke with her or a conversation. No matter how earth-shattering it was, sex was just sex. He'd better not forget it.

When he unlocked the front door, it was past eleven. A note was on the kitchen table. "Gone to bed...see you there?"

Luke ran up the stairs two at a time, hoping she wasn't asleep. He opened the bedroom door, stopped in his tracks and started to laugh, a laugh that came all the way from his belly.

"You don't laugh often enough." Katrin said, "Welcome home, Luke."

She was lying in a seductive pose on black satin sheets, wearing a sheer white nightgown that left nothing to his imagination. Red roses were strewn on the bed, while there were enough candles burning in the room to start a major fire. Marlene Dietrich was singing something sultry on the stereo; strings of tiny white lights glittered like stars all over the ceiling.

Katrin said innocently, "Did I go overboard enough? You'll notice there are no flamingos."

"Perhaps you should have included a fire extinguisher."

"The kind of fire I'm interested in can't be put out so easily," she rejoined, tossing her hair back with a gesture worthy of Dietrich.

Her nipples were pushing at the filmy white nylon, which clung to her hips and thighs. Luke said huskily, "I could help you light the fire."

"I was hoping you'd offer."

He dropped his clothes on the carpet and, naked, walked over to the bed. "As you see, I won't take much persuading."

She blushed in a very un-Dietrichlike way. "None at all, by the looks of you."

He buried his face in the softness of her breasts, her creamy skin and ardent embrace wondrously familiar. He could have told her he'd missed her; he didn't. "I hope the roses don't have thorns," he murmured; and said nothing else for quite a while.

Early the next morning Katrin and Luke boarded the first leg of a flight to Winnipeg, capital city of Manitoba. So, thought Luke, they were going back to Askja. He had no objections whatsoever; they could swim, sail and hike, and he might even get around to a little fishing.

Four days with Katrin in the village where she grew up would be just fine.

After they'd landed in Winnipeg, Katrin picked up a rental vehicle that turned out to be a four-wheel-drive wagon. She headed toward the perimeter highway that circled the city. Luke was tired; Dallas had been strenuous and he hadn't slept much the night before. "Would you mind if I have a snooze?" he asked. "I could drive after that."

"Sure," she said.

She didn't look entirely relaxed. Perhaps, he thought wryly, she was going to show him more of her past in Askja, and expected him to reciprocate. He hoped not. He'd much rather make love than war. He settled back in the seat, closed his eyes and drifted off to sleep.

He had no idea how much time had passed when he woke up. Stretching, he glanced at the clock on the dash. "Good grief, did I sleep that long? You must have worn me out last night, Katrin…we should be nearly there."

He looked around in growing puzzlement. The landscape looked both unfamiliar, yet frighteningly familiar. He said slowly, "This isn't the way to Askja."

"We're not going to Askja."

"We're in Ontario."

"Yes. We crossed the border a little while ago."

"What's up, Katrin?" Luke said tightly.

"You'll see. You agreed not to ask any questions, remember?"

He had. Relax, Luke, he told himself. Katrin doesn't know about Teal Lake. She's taking you to a resort on Lake of the Woods, that's all. He said, "Would you like me to drive?"

"No, I'm fine. If you're hungry, there are some chocolate bars and sandwiches in my pack."

He munched on a sandwich, subliminally aware that she was gripping the wheel much too tightly for someone on a perfectly innocent vacation. What was up? Why was she so tense?

He found out ten minutes later when they came to the green and white sign for Teal Lake. At the last minute

Katrin slowed, flicked on her left-hand signal and took the turnoff. Luke said sharply, "Where are we going?"

Her knuckles were now white as bone. "Teal Lake," she said. "Where else?"

"Katrin," he said in a deadly quiet voice, "turn around."

"No, Luke."

"I don't want to go anywhere near Teal Lake!"

"I'm sure you don't."

He could have grabbed the wheel. But if they both ended up in the ditch, that would solve nothing. "For the last time, turn around."

"You promised me four days of your time, no questions asked."

"I also said I loathe being manipulated," he said icily. "How did you find out about Teal Lake?"

"I had lunch with Ramon the day before you left for Dallas. He told me."

Mixed with rage was now the sharp pain of betrayal. "What did he tell you?"

"Only that the place meant something to you. Nothing more. He can be as closemouthed as you." She added with a small smile, obviously trying to lighten the atmosphere, "Although it made a change for me to ask him the questions."

The wagon was bouncing over the ruts in the dirt road. Which would, Luke knew, get worse before they got better. No wonder she'd hired a four-wheel drive. "You had this all planned, didn't you? Clever little Katrin."

A muscle twitched in her jaw. "How long will it take us to get there?"

"Oh," he said, "you'll find out." Then he leaned back in the seat and closed his eyes again. He was damned if he was going to count every tree and chunk of granite between here and their destination. Let her deal with the potholes, the culverts and washboard slopes. This was, after all, her idea.

Had he ever been so angry in his whole life?

It'd be a lifetime before he made Katrin—or any other woman—another blind promise like the one he'd made so innocently in the kitchen. He'd trusted Katrin; and she, like Ramon, had betrayed him.

He wasn't sure which was worse: anger or pain.

Time passed. The wagon lurched and bounced. Neither he nor Katrin said a word until she slowed, then turned again, this time to the right. "We're here," she said, parked the vehicle and pulled on the handbrake. Then she got out of the wagon.

Luke sat up and looked around. She'd parked at the beginning of the town. It was deserted now; the mine had closed many years ago, the inhabitants transported to other mining towns along the shield. He had two choices. He could sit here until she tired of wandering among the tumbledown buildings. Or he could join her and have the fight he was spoiling for.

He should join her anyway; this was bear country.

Luke jumped to the ground. It was late afternoon, under a clear sky. Somewhere in the woods a white-throated sparrow sang its pure, single notes, while a thrush was piping from the tall pines. The mosquitoes descended on him almost immediately. He pulled down his shirt sleeves and buttoned his collar. "So what's the plan, Katrin?" he grated. "Because I'm sure you have one."

"Let's just walk around," she said.

Her spine was like a ramrod under her cotton shirt, and she stumbled over a couple of rocks as she passed the first shack. Luke remembered it all too well. Jim Morton had lived there with his wife and half a dozen kids; the eldest boy had made Luke's life a misery until Luke had grown big enough to turn on him one day and knock him to the ground.

He, Luke, had been small for his age in those days. He'd suddenly shot up when he turned thirteen; a couple of years later, he'd lost all fear of his father.

The roof of the old country store was sagging. Like Katrin's cake, thought Luke, and heard her say, "How long since the place closed down?"

"You mean you didn't do your research?" he said nastily.

"I was hoping you'd tell me."

"You don't know me very well if you think you're going to get a guided tour."

They passed the little church, the paint peeling from its shingles, and three more houses. The windows were boarded up; desolation and abandonment hung like a miasma over the whole settlement. Gradually and inexorably grasses and shrubs were encroaching on the houses. Swallowing them, thought Luke, and wished he were anywhere else in the world but here.

They were approaching the tar-paper shack where he'd lived with his parents, and then with his father once his mother had left. His nerves had tightened to an unbearable pitch. Trying to distract himself from memories that were mobbing him like a flock of crows, he said flatly, "Why did you bring me here?"

"I thought it might open you up. Make you tell me about yourself, your parents, your past."

"Think you're pretty smart, don't you?"

She stopped right in front of his old house. "I didn't know what else to do! I can't live with someone who won't tell me the first thing about himself. You're like a medieval castle, Luke—walls ten feet thick and no windows."

"Yeah?" he said in an ugly voice, emotion seething in his chest. As though a dam had burst inside him, the words came pouring out, unstoppable, carrying everything in their path. "While we're on the subject of windows," he rasped, "why don't you take a look at the place right in front of you. That's where I grew up. You see that broken pane in the kitchen window? My dad put his fist through it one night. He was aiming at my head. But he was dead-drunk and I ducked and so he missed me. He whomped me with his belt for that...is that the kind of thing you want to know?"

Katrin paled. "Where was your mother? Couldn't she have protected you?"

"My mother took off with the local mechanic the summer I turned five. Her morals were what you might call loose...who knows if my dad really was my dad? Certainly they never bothered to get married. I was glad when she left because it meant no more fights in the middle of the night, no more broken crockery and bruises on my mother's face. How in hell could she protect me, even if she'd wanted to—she was shorter than you and my dad was a big man."

"She could have taken you with her."

"She didn't want me. To give my dad his due, he did provide me with some kind of home. At least he didn't run away like my mum. Although we were dirt poor because he drank everything he earned."

"But he used to beat you," Katrin whispered.

Her face, a frozen mask of horror, only served to make Luke angrier. "I learned very young to stay out in the woods all night if he'd been into the booze, and I was always quicker on my feet than him. But sometimes he caught me, yeah. So are you getting the picture? Can you see why I'm not rushing you to the altar, or fathering a dozen kids? I never want to have children!"

"That's why you've made so much money...so you'll

never be poor again," she said in a dazed voice. "Where's your father now, Luke?"

"When I turned fifteen, he took his belt off once too often. I flattened him against the wall and told him I'd beat the tar out of him if he ever tried that again. The next morning I left. Went north. I lied about my age, worked the mines and started saving money."

"Did you ever come back here?"

"Never. I got word two years later that he'd died of a heart attack…there was no reason to come back."

"So you never made peace with him."

Luke's throat tightened; to his horror he felt tears sting his eyes. With a tiny sound of compassion, Katrin stepped closer and tried to put her arms around him. He struck her away. "I've always regretted that I never came back here, or tried to meet my dad on a more even footing. Not everyone saddled with a rebellious kid who might not even be his own flesh and blood would have hung in like my dad did. But I never told him that. And now it's too late. Years too late."

He, Luke, could have ended up in an orphanage; and rough though his upbringing had been, Luke knew in his bones that an orphanage would have stifled him. His fists clenched at his sides, he went on, "There was more to my dad than the booze and his belt. His whole life he worked to get unions into the mines. Every mine I own is unionized, and the safety regulations are strictly adhered to or I close the place down…it's the least I can do for him."

"It's a fine legacy," Katrin said unsteadily.

"Maybe he loved my mum, despite her infidelities. Maybe that's why he drank. Or maybe it was because of his own childhood—he came over here from the slums of Glasgow, God knows what his upbringing was like. There's so much I never asked him. And now I can't."

Katrin was gazing at the little house as though it might

tell her all its secrets. "Wasn't there anyone here who loved you? Someone you could run to when you were in trouble?"

"Me? Run for help? Not likely," Luke said ironically. "You asked me once what my middle name was. How about independence?"

"You have two middle names," Katrin said with a flare of her normal spirit. "The second one's pride."

She'd got that right. "You think I was going to tell the whole village what my life was like? How terrified I was sometimes? How lonely I felt, how unloved?" He gave a derisive laugh. "There are worse things than the occasional night in the woods."

"You've never told anyone any of this."

"Imagine that."

"Not everyone's like your parents!"

"Right," he said sarcastically, raking his fingers through his hair. "Have you seen enough? Or do we have to walk the whole goddamned street?"

"I've seen enough."

"Good. Then let's get out of here."

Katrin dragged her eyes away from the rotting wooden gutters, where flaps of tar paper hung from the roof. In a low voice she said, "I brought you here for another reason."

"I think you've done enough damage for one day."

"I didn't mean to hurt you! I needed to know more about you, to try and understand you. To get behind all those barriers you hide behind."

"Why do you need to do that?" he exploded. "What business is it of yours?"

She drew in a ragged breath. "Haven't you guessed?" she said. "I'm in love with you, Luke."

CHAPTER FIFTEEN

INTO the silence came the whitethroat's clear lament, piercingly sweet. Luke said with careful restraint, "Would you mind repeating that?"

"You heard," Katrin said with a touch of desperation. "I love you. I've been in love with you for weeks, that's why I was so devastated when you left in the middle of the night after we first made love. That's why I want more of you than you're giving me. Don't get me wrong, I love how we are in bed together, it's truly wonderful. But it's not enough. I can't build a relationship on sex, Luke. There has to be more than that."

His heart felt like a chunk of ice. The lake used to freeze solid every winter, he remembered absently, that's when he'd learned how to skate. He said flatly, "You've ruined everything."

"Don't say that!"

"I don't know how to love. And I don't want to learn. Not with you. Not with anyone. It's too late."

She said with passionate conviction, "It's never too late to learn how to love someone. Never."

"Then sooner or later you'll learn to love someone else, won't you?" he blazed. "Because I'm not available. Will you get that through your head?"

"I don't want someone else. I want you."

"Then you're a fool," Luke grated, too angry to care what he said. "I've had enough of this. As far as I'm concerned, you've forfeited your other three days—I want to go straight back to the airport. You can come back to San Francisco with me or not, as you please. If you do, I'll be faithful to you and I'll put you through law school. But I won't fall in love with you and I won't marry you.''

''And you won't take me on business trips, don't forget that,'' she flared. ''Let's go—we can't get to the airport soon enough for me.''

She marched ahead of him down the dirt road, her hips swinging in her cotton trousers, one hand slapping at a mosquito on the back of her neck. Luke took off after her, swung her around, planted a furious kiss on her parted lips, and snarled, ''I'm doing the driving. I've had enough surprises for one day.''

''You can do what you damn well please!''

Her eyes were as turbulent as an ocean storm; she looked so beautiful that he had to bite back the one question he refused to ask. Whether she was coming back to San Francisco with him or not.

If she was in love with him, it would be better if she didn't. He said furiously, ''I'll tell you one thing—you don't look like you're in love with me. You look like you hate my guts.''

''How would you know what love looks like?''

How indeed? ''Give me the keys to the wagon,'' he ordered. She hauled them out of her pocket, dropped them on his palm without touching him, and kept on walking.

He didn't want to look at the houses, or the pale beauty of the evening sky. He certainly didn't want to look at Katrin. Never so glad in his life to get behind the wheel of a vehicle, Luke snapped his seat belt and took off in a spurt of gravel.

Two hours later, during which neither he nor Katrin had said a single word to each other, they arrived at the airport. Katrin said with icy precision, ''You can stop at the arrivals area. I'm staying here.''

In his heart Luke had known that would be her decision. But not for the richest gold mine in the world would he tell her how it stabbed him to the core, cutting through anger as though it were water. "Fine," he said.

He skirted the brick buildings, pulling up outside the international entrance. Flicking the button for the trunk, so he could get out his bag, he left the engine running. "Goodbye, Katrin," he said.

What else could he add? That said it all.

She blurted, "If you change your mind, will you get in touch with me?"

His jaw tightened. "Don't hold your breath."

"In the long run, you're the loser here."

"That's only your opinion," he said and got out of the wagon. He took his duffel bag from the trunk, slammed it shut and walked through the glass doors without a second look. Only when he got to the counter did he glance back. The wagon was gone.

Katrin was gone. Katrin, who was in love with him.

When Luke got home the next day, he went through his house from top to bottom, getting rid of every trace of Katrin's presence. Her clothes, including the feathered dress, he packed in a box to send to her, along with her cosmetics, and a couple of books she'd bought. His face set, he took the black satin sheets off the bed, tossing them in the box, too. He hung fresh towels in the bathroom, putting the ones she'd used into the washer. Finally he cleaned out the food she'd left in the refrigerator, and threw the drooping red roses and the candle stubs into the garbage as well.

If only he could exorcise her from his head as easily.

He kept expecting her to come running down the stairs, smiling at him with that warmth that he now knew sprang from loving him. If only she hadn't been so stupid as to fall in love. If only they could have gone on as they were…

Swearing under his breath, Luke taped up the box and

addressed it to her in Askja. He hadn't put a note inside. What was there to say?

They'd both said too much. Words that couldn't be taken back.

It was a relief to leave the box at the post office the next morning on his way to work; and even more of a relief to go back to the office, where immediately he was submerged in the innumerable details of his various projects. If any of his staff wondered why he'd come back from vacation early, one look at his face would have discouraged them from asking.

He looked awful.

It was a case of too much emotion and a sleepless night. He'd get over it.

But a week later Luke looked worse, with his eyes dark-shadowed and new lines around his mouth. Nor had his sleep patterns improved. No matter how much he told himself it was only sexual deprivation, he was still haunted by dreams: erotic dreams and dreams of loss that figured a woman with blond hair smooth as a river. Equally bad were nightmares about his father, suffused with the same leaden and unredeemable regret.

In the bright sun or beneath the white clouds of a San Francisco September day, Luke could persuade himself these were only dreams; but at night he couldn't as easily shake them off.

He hadn't gotten in touch with Ramon, still bothered by a sense of betrayal. When Ramon phoned him at work exactly eight days after his return, and suggested lunch, Luke agreed with an inner reluctance he did his best to conceal. They met in their favorite Thai restaurant, ordering curried *mat saman* and beer. Ramon raised his glass. "I've been meaning to call you for several days, Luke. But a new case took over and there's been no time." He took a long gulp. "I need to say this to you face-to-face—I told Katrin nothing but the name Teal Lake and the fact that you and I had had boyhoods that were far from ideal.''

"You sure get right to the point."

"You're my friend." Ramon shrugged. "And life is short. Too short for misunderstandings. A couple of weeks ago she phoned me at work and asked if we could meet for lunch. It was then that she asked me if I knew anything about your childhood. I could have told her nothing. I weighed that against the way your tennis has gone downhill, and decided to tell her the absolute minimum. But by the look of you, I shouldn't have.''

"We went to Teal Lake," Luke said. "She and I. It was a disaster. I haven't seen her since, nor will I.''

Ramon raised his brow. "I repeat…life is short, too short for misunderstandings.''

"She says she's in love with me. I can't handle that. So I backed off. That's not what I'd call a misunderstanding.''

The waiter put spring rolls and peanut sauce in front of them. Thoughtfully Ramon began to eat. "The price of gold and precious metals is down. Is that why you look like a whipped cur?''

"What other reason?"

"Rosita wants you to come to the house tonight," Ramon added casually. "She's making tamales.''

Three or four times Luke had eaten Rosita's fiery and delicious Mexican food. "You know I can't turn that invitation down.''

"Good. Six o'clock? You know the way." Ramon then began to discuss an interesting new development in lie detection. To Luke's relief, Teal Lake wasn't mentioned again.

Promptly at six, Luke presented himself at Ramon and Rosita's Victorian house on the western edge of the Mission District, a vibrantly Hispanic area of the city. He'd always enjoyed his visits here, entering the alien world of a close-knit family, then returning to his house afterward with secret pleasure that it was so quiet and peaceful. Rosita opened the door with a welcoming smile. "Come in, Luke."

She was tall, her jet-black hair a tumble of curls around a face as beautiful and full of character in its own way as Katrin's was. As he passed her a bottle of red wine from his cellars, she said, "*Gracias*... we're eating right away, the children have to go to bed early as it's a school night."

She led him into the kitchen, with its terra-cotta tiles. Copper pans and bunched herbs hung from the beamed ceiling. The oak table in the alcove was set with Mexican woven mats; the shutters were closed, giving an artificial dimness. Felipe, who was seven, was lighting tall white tapers with an air of intense concentration; Constancia, a year younger, was arranging some rather tattered daisies as a centerpiece. Maria, aged three, ran over to Luke, grabbed him around the knees, and crowed, "Lift me, lift me."

They'd played this game before, although the last time was probably three months ago. Touched that she'd remembered, Luke swung her chubby little body high over his head, almost to the oak beams. Then he swooped her down again. She shrieked with delight. "More, more!"

Her weight, her gleeful chortle and unselfconscious delight filled Luke with a sudden, devastating poignancy. He'd always closed himself off from the possibility of having children of his own; it wasn't in the cards. But tonight, Katrin's absence was like an open wound and he was achingly aware of another lack: that no child of his would ever run to him, trustingly, like Maria.

His child and Katrin's?

"Do it again!" Maria shrieked.

With a start, Luke came back to the present. Was he seriously contemplating fatherhood? Which, in his books, would require marriage as the prerequisite. He gave his head a stunned shake, quite unaware that Ramon was watching him from the corner of the room, looking rather pleased with himself.

After one last swoop through the air, Luke put Maria down on the tiled floor. Shy Constancia favored Luke with her grave smile. Felipe, whose present ambition was to be a racing driver, asked about his sports car. Ramon, in a T-shirt and jeans, poured the wine, and Rosita brought the food to the table.

The untidy, laughter-filled kitchen was like a haven, thought Luke. Katrin would like the Torres family. He pushed this insight away as Felipe said grace in Spanish and they all began to eat, the candles illuminating the circle of faces. Luke ate too much, the wine slipping down easily; afterward, he and Ramon cleaned up the dishes while Rosita got the children ready for bed. As he always did, Luke read all three children a story, then said good night to them.

As he softly closed Felipe's door, Luke was visited again by that disturbing sense of poignancy. He'd always assumed that because of his upbringing, he'd make a lousy father. After all, what kind of a model had he had? But maybe he'd underestimated himself. Maybe he'd be okay.

A daughter or a son of his own. Would they be dark-haired like himself? Or blond and blue-eyed like Katrin?

I never want children. That's what he'd told her. Children or marriage or commitment. And so he'd driven her away.

He needed three hard sets of tennis. That's what he needed. Kids and marriage and love…what did he know about all that?

Rosita left for a class she was taking at the art school; Ramon poured glasses of tequila and the two men watched part of a basketball game on TV. Luke could see Ramon was tired; about nine, he stood up. "I'm off. Thanks so much, Ramon."

Ramon stood up, too. "A word, Luke," he said with an odd formality, "before you go. Over the years, we have never talked about the things that happened to us as little boys. Young like Felipe. But this evening I need to speak about it."

"Not on my account, you don't."

"Yes," Ramon said, "on your account. Our friendship is too important for me to stay silent."

Luke tugged at the neck of his sweater. "I don't need any lectures, Ramon, no matter how well-meant. I'm doing fine."

Ramon said curtly, "Shut up, *amigo,* and listen."

Ramon had never used that tone of voice to Luke before; not for the first time, Luke understood how the other man had risen from a rookie on the beat to his present position. He, Luke, could have responded in kind—he was no slouch in that department himself—but he realized he was curious to hear what Ramon had to say. "Okay," he said, "I'll shut up."

"At Felipe's age," Ramon began, "I was just one more street kid in Mexico City. Scavenging for food, staying one step ahead of the law." For a moment he was silent, his dark eyes lost in the past. Then he picked up the thread again. "I had *machismo.* I knew how to steal and shoplift, how to wire cars and pick locks...and I never got caught. Just as well, or I wouldn't have made it into the police force. I am a good policeman. I know the other side, you see." Ramon grinned. "When I was eighteen, I met Rosita. I wanted her, *Dios,* how I wanted her. But she told me I had to go straight, get a job...and then, maybe, she would let me into her bed."

Forgetting his ill-temper, Luke said intuitively, "I bet you ran away as if the devil was at your heels."

Ramon chuckled. "For ten months, I stayed away. But she was my fate, Luke, my destiny. So I got a job at the fish market, I went to night school, and the rest is history."

"Are you trying to tell me Katrin's my fate?" Luke said quizzically.

"I'm telling you she's a remarkable woman. I saw her under the worst of circumstances, so I know. And you are a good man. Don't run away from her as I did from Rosita. Marry her, have children, fill that empty house on the hill with love...if I can do it, so can you. And now I'm going to end this so solemn sermon, and I will never mention my childhood again."

He clapped Luke on the shoulder, and said good night. Luke drove home. On his way upstairs he went into the kitchen to put a couple of tamales Rosita had given him into the refrigerator. The kitchen was clean, sterile, and silent as the grave. Is that what he wanted for the rest of his life? To be half alive?

He walked upstairs, in no hurry to get to his empty bedroom. He and Ramon had been friends for many years; for the first time ever, Luke found himself envying Ramon the laughter, intimacy and tangible love that had filled every corner of the old Victorian house. Ramon would never make a fortune, as Luke had. But maybe Ramon had something far more precious, that money couldn't buy. A wife who adored him. Children who loved him.

And Ramon in turn adored Rosita, loved his children, would protect them with his last breath.

Just as Luke had wanted to protect Katrin.

He sank down on the bed, gazing at the patch of carpet where Katrin's feathered dress had fallen in a crumpled heap. He couldn't live with her. He couldn't live without her.

Classic.

What was he going to do?

He could pick up the phone. Speak to her. Tell her he missed her. That he was no longer self-sufficient. That his whole life was out of whack and only she could fix it.

This was nothing to do with love. But maybe it was a start.

CHAPTER SIXTEEN

BEFORE he could change his mind, Luke reached for the telephone, absently noticing that the red message signal was flashing. It wouldn't be Katrin; she was too proud to get in touch with him after he'd made it so abundantly clear he didn't want anything to do with her unless it was on his terms. He dialed her number quickly, waiting for her to answer, his heart racing.

It rang four times. Then her voice, calm and impersonal, told him he could leave a message at the sound of the beep and she'd get back to him as soon as possible.

She wasn't home.

He had no idea where she was. But surely she hadn't left Askja permanently; the phone would be disconnected if she had.

He put the receiver down without leaving a message. Aware of a crushing disappointment, he rested his head in his hands. What had he expected? That the moment he phoned her, she'd be there waiting for him?

How arrogant was that?

Desperate for something to do, Luke entered the password to his voice mail. A woman's voice started speaking. "This is Anna Bendickt, from Askja...we met briefly at Margret's tearoom, I'm Lara and Tomas's mother... I have some bad news. Katrin is very ill...she doesn't know I'm phoning you. She's in hospital in Winnipeg with pneumonia, she had an accident in her daysailer. If you want more information, you can phone me." She then gave the name of the hospital, and her own phone number. Her voice, Luke noticed, wasn't overly friendly. But why would it be?

After the second attempt, he managed to put the receiver back in its cradle. His hands were shaking as if he had a tremor. Katrin was ill. So ill that Anna, who must thoroughly dislike him for the way he'd treated Katrin, had been impelled to call him.

He had to see Katrin. Luke gripped his knees hard, trying to still his trembling fingers. If he'd needed proof that she meant something to him, something of deep significance, he now had it. But was the terror he was feeling a measure of love?

He didn't know what love was.

What if he lost Katrin before he had the chance to tell her how important she was to him? To apologize for being such a stubborn fool?

What if he was too late?

Think, Luke. Think.

His company jet, which had been in east Africa when he and Katrin had flown to Manitoba, was now here, at the airport. Swiftly he phoned the pilot and made the necessary arrangements. Then he phoned the hospital, and after a series of delays, spoke to the floor supervisor for respiratory diseases. "My name's Luke MacRae," he said, "I'm calling from San Francisco. I'm a good friend of Katrin Sigurdson's, I only just found out she's ill."

"Her condition is quite serious, Mr. MacRae…to put it bluntly, she's not putting up much of a fight." The supervisor gave a few details, then added, "If you can do anything to improve matters, I'd suggest you come very soon."

"I will," Luke said hoarsely. "I'll get there as quickly as I can. Thank you."

Nothing his father had ever done had induced in him such dread as he was feeling now. He threw a few clothes into an overnight bag, left a message at the office, and ran downstairs to the garage. His whole body was focussed on one thing and one thing only: to see Katrin. To instill in her the will to fight.

She loved him. He'd turned her away. Was that why she lacked the will to live?

Was love that powerful?

It was still dark when Luke got to the hospital. The taxi dropped him at the front door. He hurried inside, was given directions to the floor he needed and took the elevator. It moved with agonizing slowness.

Once the jet had taken off from the Winnipeg airport, Luke had spoken to Anna. Katrin, so Anna had said, had overturned the daysailer, fallen into the cold waters of the lake, and within a few days had succumbed to a bronchial infection that turned into full-blown pneumonia. Anna herself had been at the hospital, but had had to return home because her elderly mother had come down with the flu. At the end of the conversation, Luke had said awkwardly, "Thank you for letting me know, Anna."

"I'm glad you'll be with her," Anna said stiffly. "If— when she regains consciousness, give her my love."

"When. Not if," Luke said forcibly. "And, yes, I will."

He'd also phoned the hospital, to be told Katrin was no better and no worse.

The elevator doors slid open with a metallic sigh. Luke marched to the desk, and was directed to Katrin's room. A nurse was sitting quietly by the bed. But Luke's eyes went straight to the woman in the bed.

Beneath a crisp white coverlet, Katrin was lying very still, except for the labored exhalations of her breathing. Intravenous tubes were delivering saline and antibiotics through her left arm. Her cheeks were flushed, and when he reached out his hand and rested it on her forehead, it was burningly hot. Her hair was damp with sweat.

Luke pulled up a chair and sat down. He clasped her

hand in his, gently stroking her palm; it had been a private signal of theirs, an acknowledgment of the physical closeness they'd so often shared.

Pain clenched his heart. Forgetting the nurse's presence almost immediately, he focused his whole being on Katrin, bringing all his willpower to bear on her. Very softly he said, "Katrin, it's Luke. I'm here, with you. I should never have left you, I'm more sorry than I can say for doing that to you. But I'm here, right now, and I'm not going away until your fever's gone and you're over the worst. You're going to get better, Katrin, of course you are...your whole life is ahead of you."

He talked on and on, telling her about his evening with Ramon and Rosita, describing what Ramon had said; and finding in the darkness the courage to express how he valued this friendship between two strong-minded men. He told her about Felipe, Constancia and Maria; he described Rosita's fiery temperament and equally inflammatory enchiladas. And from there, he started to talk more fully about his childhood years with all their loneliness and fear.

But there had been more to Teal Lake than unhappiness, and Luke told her about that, too. The eagles that had arrived every September; the moose and deer in the woods, the shy black bears, and the mountain lion he had once sighted on a granite outcrop. Wild blueberries and raspberries, spruce gum, drinking from the clear streams of the backwoods, he described them all.

The nurses changed shifts. Someone brought him some very strong tea and a sugared doughnut. His cell phone rang twice, both times from the office with news of two crises, one in central Africa, the other in Malaysia. And still Luke talked.

Katrin was moving restlessly in the bed now, her cheeks hectically flushed. A doctor arrived, made noncommittal noises, and left. Intuitively Luke knew the medical staff was doing all that could be done; it was up to Katrin now.

It was up to him.

He got up from the chair for a few minutes, splashed cold water on his face in the bathroom, and stretched. Then he sat down again, taking both her hands in his, resting his cheek against her smooth skin. "Katrin," he whispered, "you must get well. I need you."

For the second time since he'd met her, tears stung his eyes. "I need you," he repeated. And then Luke heard himself say the words he'd never believed he'd say to any woman. "I love you, Katrin."

The words replayed in his mind, such simple words with such enormous portent. Then his heart leaped in his chest. Had her fingers moved ever so slightly? Or had he imagined it? Imagined it because he so desperately needed a sign of hope, a signal that at some level she was hearing him?

He raised his head, saying more strongly, "Katrin, I love you. I'm sorry it's taken me this long to figure it out, more sorry than I can say. But it's true…I love you. I want you, I need you, you must get well so we can be together."

In his pocket, his cell phone rang. He shut it off impatiently, all his attention on the woman lying in the bed. The woman he loved with all his heart.

Briefly he dropped his forehead to her hands again, his whole body suffused with this new knowledge, so inescapable, so full of the unknown. What would it mean to him? How could he possibly guess? She had to get better, so he could find out what it was like to love a woman. A woman who loved him back.

Perhaps, he thought humbly, he was about to embark on the greatest adventure of his life.

Again Luke focussed every ounce of his energy on Katrin and her struggle for life, willing her to feel his presence through the fever that claimed her. The seconds turned to minutes, to an hour. Then the doctor returned, asked Luke to leave the room, and within a few minutes came back out. "Well," he said, "I don't know what you did, but she's over the hump...the fever's broken. She should regain consciousness within the next few hours. Good work."

He ambled off, an older man who looked as though, like Luke, he'd been up all night. Leaning against the wall, Luke watched him go. Katrin was going to recover. That's what he'd said. She was going to be all right.

Luke sagged against the pale green paint, aware of a deep exhaustion in every fiber of his body. He'd never wanted anything—money, power, prestige—as much as he wanted Katrin to get well. Nor ever would.

He'd crossed a watershed in the last few hours. And there was no going back.

Pushing himself away from the wall, he went back in the room. The nurse smiled at him. "I'll be leaving now that she's over the worst." She patted him on the sleeve. "Very good news."

"Yes," Luke said blankly, "it is. Thanks for everything you've done."

"I think you did more than I did," said the nurse, and left the room.

Luke sank down on the chair, not sure he had the energy to stand up. Katrin looked different, he gradually realized. Her cheeks were a softer pink, her breathing less labored. The doctor was right: she was going to recover.

For a long time Luke simply sat there, allowing simple gratitude to work its way through his tired mind. Eventually he reached in his pocket for the mints he kept there, knowing he should go to the cafeteria and eat something more substantial, yet reluctant to leave her. His hand bumped against his cell phone. When he turned it back on, it started to flash imperiously.

The crises, he learned as he listened to the messages from two of his senior assistants, had worsened. There was a strike in the mine in central Africa, and much worse, a serious accident in his new mine in Malaysia. Several miners were trapped, some feared dead.

Ever since the mining accident in Teal Lake that had killed eleven men the summer Luke was six, he'd had a dread of such occurrences; and, as an adult, a lasting sense of responsibility toward them. He should be there, he thought, on site. Making sure that everything that humanly could be done was being done.

But that meant he'd have to leave Katrin before she regained consciousness. Leave her without telling her to her face that he loved her.

He walked out of the room again, spoke to both his assistants, and then to the pilot at the Winnipeg airport. He delegated the strike, but he had to go to Malaysia himself. He'd always put the safety and well-being of his miners before profits, a stance that had sometimes gotten him in trouble with his stockholders. He couldn't change that now. Honor was a very old-fashioned concept. But his honor was at stake here.

He could explain to Katrin. Surely, when she heard about the underground explosion and the trapped miners, she'd understand.

Quickly he scribbled a note to her, explaining what was going on. But then his pen stopped, digging into the paper. He could sign it *love, Luke*. Or he could just sign it *Luke*.

Luke, he wrote, and tore the paper from the pad. He wanted to say that word to her first, rather than write it. It was too basic to be scrawled on a scrap of paper and left at her bedside.

Back in the room, he put the note prominently on the

stand that held her personal effects; he'd tell the nurses it was there, to make sure she got it. Then he leaned over, kissed Katrin's blessedly cool cheek and said softly, "I'll be back. I love you, Katrin. More than I can say."

An hour later he was on his way to Malaysia.

The next day, from halfway around the world, Luke managed to speak to Katrin. She sounded very tired; she also sounded more distant than the miles between them warranted. He said clumsily, "Did you get my note?"

"Yes, I did."

"It's a waiting game here, Katrin. They're tunneling through solid rock to get to the trapped men, I don't feel I can leave until we know more."

"Of course not."

"You do understand?"

"Oh, yes," she said, an indecipherable note in her voice.

"How are you feeling?"

"I'm as weak as a newborn kitten. Otherwise fine. They're saying I can go home tomorrow."

"Already?"

"They need the bed for someone sicker than me."

"Katrin, I—" Luke broke off. The words that had come so easily to his lips when she was lying there unconscious were now lodged somewhere in his larynx. Stuck like a fishbone.

I love you. Why couldn't he say it? What kind of a man was he? It wasn't that he no longer felt it, that wasn't the issue. He longed to be with her, to touch her, hold her, pour out everything that was in his heart.

That was it. He needed to be face-to-face with her in order to say those three small, so important words. "Will Anna be able to look in on you when you're back home?" he asked.

"I'm sure she will. Her mother's feeling better already."

"I wish to God I was there," he exploded.

The line crackled. Katrin said nothing. Cursing himself for being so inept, Luke retreated to familiar territory, describing the situation at the pithead more fully. Then he said with sudden urgency, "I've got to go, the foreman's signaling. Bye, Katrin, I'll call you tomorrow."

"I could be in transit tomorrow," she said with that same daunting politeness. "Goodbye, Luke."

The connection was broken. Luke shoved the phone in his pocket. Everything would be all right once he saw her.

He'd waited thirty-four years to say I love you. Another week wasn't going to make any difference.

CHAPTER SEVENTEEN

JUST over a week later Luke was on his way back to Winnipeg. They'd been able to rescue all but five of the miners. He'd stayed for the funerals, and to ensure that everything possible would be done for the families of the dead men. He hadn't talked to Katrin for the last three days; she hadn't been home and hadn't responded to any of his messages.

He was desperate to see her.

Why hadn't she gotten in touch with him?

He showered on the jet, changed into clean clothes and decided that the bush gear he'd been wearing for what felt like the whole time should probably be incinerated. He then shaved, avoiding the ugly gash in his cheek that he'd gotten at the mine face. After he'd eaten, he tried very hard to catch up on some sleep; but he was too wired to sleep. Until he was holding Katrin in his arms, he couldn't relax or sleep. It was that simple.

Or that complicated.

The flight seemed to take forever. But finally, after three stopovers for refueling and customs, Luke was running down the steps toward the car waiting for him on the tarmac. He got in, consulted the map briefly, and headed north out of the city. He'd tried to reach Anna, when he'd been unsuccessful in talking to Katrin, but with no better luck.

He could be on a wild-goose chase. Maybe Katrin was no longer in Askja.

He should have told her on the phone that he loved her, should have forgotten all his scruples about being face-to-face with her. As far as she knew, he was still totally averse to falling in love, or to commitment of any kind.

He'd been a stupid jerk.

If she wasn't in Askja, he thought grimly, he'd follow her to the ends of the earth. Because that, so he was learning, was what love was all about.

When Luke reached the little village, he went first to Katrin's house. But when he banged on the side door and then rang the front doorbell, there was no response. Her car wasn't parked in the driveway or in the run-down garage. Anxiety thrumming along his nerves, he drove to the resort. Katrin's car wasn't in the staff parking lot, either. He then traveled the length of the village to Anna's house.

Anna was out in the garden, wearing a jacket against the cool knife of wind from the lake. Luke got out of the car and walked toward her. She watched him, unsmiling, her garden gloves caked with dirt. "Anna," he said, "I know I've been behaving like a prize idiot. But if I can, I've come here to make amends. Katrin's car's gone. Do you know where she is?"

"She's gone camping."

"Where? Do you know?"

"After today, are you going to get in your car and drive away again?" Anna demanded. "Leaving her alone?"

"I want to marry her," Luke said.

Of course he did. That's why he'd come all this way.

"Oh." Anna's smile was quick and generous. "Well, then. She's gone north of here. If you have a map, I can show you."

She stripped off her muddy gloves, and traced the route Luke should take. "I didn't want her to go. The nights are cold, and she's still not quite back to normal. But you know Katrin, she can be very stubborn."

"Like me," Luke said wryly, folding the map so he could see the relevant section of the lakeshore. He then added with awkward sincerity, "Thank you, Anna. If Katrin will have me, I swear I'll do my best to make her happy."

"Start by persuading her to give up this camping foolishness. Or," Anna's smile was demure, "find a way of keeping her warm."

Abruptly realizing that he liked Anna very much, Luke laughed. "I'll see what I can do. Wish me luck."

He then got in his car and drove north. The highway followed the shoreline, the lake sometimes hidden by trees, at other times stretching to the horizon with the dull gleam of pewter. It was going to be dark by the time he got there; he only hoped he could locate Katrin's campsite.

He finally arrived at the little provincial park whose name Anna had given him. There was a map of all the campsites at the kiosk; but because it was late in the season, the kiosk was empty. A hand-printed sign asked him to choose his own campsite and pay in the morning.

Luke took a copy of the map and started driving along the narrow dirt road. Most of the sites were empty, although there were a few trailers lined up to one side. He followed the curve of the road, passed several empty sites, then saw Katrin's car parked at the most secluded end of the campground. He parked in the next site, got out and locked his car. Doing up his jacket, he started down the little slope that led to the lake.

He halted briefly. Tucked in a small hollow, sheltered from the wind, was a green dome tent. He called Katrin's name softly, not wanting to scare her, and walked up to it. It was then that he saw, down by the lakeshore, the flicker of flames. His shoes slipping on the pine needles, he walked closer, stopping so that he was partly hidden by the trunk of a tall pine.

Overhead the needled boughs of the pine and the golden leaves of poplars rustled secretively. Waves lapped on the stones. From deeper in the forest an owl hooted, rhythmically and repetitively. Then the hair rose on the back of Luke's neck. Far across the lake a wolf howled, the prolonged and infinitely lonely voice of the wilderness.

Katrin was sitting on a boulder by the fire, her back to the lake. She was feeding twigs to the flames. She looked very unhappy. But more than unhappy, Luke decided slowly. The slump of her shoulders, the downward curve of her lips spoke of defeat.

Defeated? His strong and courageous Katrin?

Even as he watched, she stood up, turning to face the water. She was wearing a dark red fleece jacket, hiking boots on her feet, her hair in a thick braid down her back. She leaned against the trunk of a poplar, then suddenly bowed her head as though she were crying.

She never cried.

He couldn't stand seeing her like this, so isolated and unhappy. Luke shuffled his feet in the underbrush, dislodging some rocks that skittered down the slope, and called out her name.

She whirled, staring upward beyond the circle of flame into the darkness. Swiping at her cheeks, she said sharply, "Who's there?"

"It's me. Luke," he said, and loped down the slope toward her. "I'm sorry, I didn't mean to frighten you."

"I'm not frightened," she said, standing very straight. "How did you find me here?"

"Anna told me where you were."

"Some friend she is," Katrin said bitterly. "Why don't you turn right around and go back where you came from, Luke MacRae? After all, that's what you do best."

"I know you must think that. But—"

"I can't bear you wandering in and out of my life like this!" she flared. "You were at the hospital, I know you were. But did you hang around long enough to talk to me once I'd regained consciousness? Oh no, you took off again. Because someone called you from work. After all, compared to a Malaysian mine, who am I? You know where your priorities are, and they sure don't have my name on them. It's not good enough, Luke, I won't put myself through this over and over again. I won't, do you hear me?''

"That's all changed—"

He might just as well not have spoken. Her words tumbling over one another, she went on, "You don't know how often I've regretted telling you I loved you. I've made some big mistakes in my life, Donald being one of them. But saying I'd fallen for you was even stupider than marrying Donald—it was a licence for you to walk all over me.''

Stung, Luke said, "I've never walked all over you!''

"Great-aunt Gudrun brought me up to believe in honesty. Well, Great-aunt Gudrun was wrong. There are times when saying what's on your mind is a shortcut to disaster.''

Luke clenched his fists at his side. "Have you changed your mind?'' he croaked. "Don't you love me anymore?''

"That's none of your business!''

Desperate to know the answer, Luke stepped out of the shadows and into the open, his face illumined by the orange glow of the flames. In a shocked voice Katrin said, "What happened to your face?''

He put a hand up to the scrape on his cheek; the bruise underlying it was now an ugly purple-yellow. "It's nothing.''

"What happened? Tell me.''

"I went down in the mine with the rescue team,'' Luke said impatiently. "I always do. There was a minor rockslide, that's when I got hit. But we all got out with no trouble, and the next day they were able to break through and rescue the miners who were still alive.''

"You could have been killed,'' she whispered.

"Well, I wasn't." Now that he'd started, he seemed unable to stop. "When I was six, there was an accident in the mine at Teal Lake, before it was unionized or there were proper safety measures. I've never forgotten it—my dad's drinking got worse after that, and why not? So I feel responsible if ever there are accidents in the mines that I own. A few of the guys at the conferences laugh at me for that. But they're laughing at the wrong man."

"In so many ways, Teal Lake has made you what you are," Katrin said slowly. "For better and for worse."

"I went to the hospital the minute I heard you were ill," Luke said violently. "I stayed the rest of the night and into the next day, until your fever broke and the doctors said you were going to be okay. I got the message about the mine explosion shortly after I got to the hospital. But I ignored it, Katrin. Until you were out of danger, I put you first. You're the only woman I've ever done that for."

"I knew you were there," she said. "Don't ask me how I knew, when I wasn't even conscious. But I knew. When I came to and you were gone... I was so bitterly disappointed, it was terrible. Oh, Luke, I know I blew it taking you to Teal Lake. But what else was I to do? How else could I have broken through to you?"

"I don't know what else you could have done."

Her smile was wobbly. "That's a huge admission."

"Yeah...but I'd never told anyone about all the stuff that went on there. About my mother, my father and his drinking, my loneliness and isolation. Afterward, I felt naked. Stripped. Flayed. I couldn't bear to be around you. So I took off faster than a bat out of hell. And for that I'm sorry."

"And then you took off again, from the hospital. You can't keep doing this to me."

The strain in her voice hurt him deep inside, in a place he'd always kept separate. "But I've changed," he said roughly. "I've realized something. Something that's been staring me in the face for days. For weeks." Hadn't he come here just to tell her these three small words? And now that the moment had arrived, Luke found it unexpectedly easy. "I love you," he said. "Katrin, I love you."

The owl hooted again, closer this time. Katrin thrust her hands in her pockets. "You said you didn't know how to love anyone. And you weren't interested in learning."

"I said a lot that day at Teal Lake that I regret."

"I won't settle for being on the sidelines of your life. Someone you turn on and off, as it suits you. I want the whole man."

His nails digging into his palms, Luke asked the crucial question. "Do you still love me? Or have I destroyed that, too? Because I'm the one who's responsible for you ending up in hospital."

"You weren't responsible for me falling into the lake," she said roundly. "There was a freak storm, no one predicted it. But at the hospital... I was just so tired, I didn't have the energy to fight. Yet once you arrived, I somehow knew you were there, holding my hand, talking to me. So you saved my life, Luke. That's what you did."

"I talked more that night than the rest of my life put together. I told you everything I could think of about Teal Lake. Then I talked about Ramon and his wife and kids. At the end, I even told you I loved you." His voice roughened. "But when we talked on the phone the next day—I couldn't get the words out. I knew I had to be face-to-face with you. Because they're the three most important words in the world."

She bit her lip. "For me they are."

"Katrin, I have to know—do you still love me?"

Her eyes were dark pools, black as the night. A waft of smoke blew across her face, as at her feet a pile of twigs collapsed in a crackle of orange and red. She said quietly,

"Love can't be destroyed so easily…yes, I love you, Luke. I always will."

He let out his breath in a long sigh. "I don't know the first thing about love," he said. "But I can learn. You could teach me. Because there's one more thing I haven't said. The most important of all. I want you to marry me, Katrin. Be my wife."

"You *do?*"

"I want the whole deal," Luke said, his eyes intent on her face. "A proper wedding, you always by my side. Living with me, traveling with me, being with me. Day and night."

"Oh, Luke," she said unsteadily, "when you do something, you do it wholeheartedly."

He closed the distance between them, putting his arms around her waist and pulling her to the length of his body. "Marry me? Because I love you more than I can say."

Her smile glimmered amidst the sheen of tears in her eyes. "One condition," she said.

He grinned. "Conditions, huh? I've already told you you're more important that fifty mines."

"Your house," she said. "You've got to sell it—I don't want to live in a concrete box."

He threw back his head and laughed. "We'll live wherever you like, my darling."

"You've never called me that before," she said shakily.

"Dearest, darling and most adorable Katrin, I love you," Luke said. "The house'll be on the market quicker than you spilled brandy on Guy Wharton."

Her smile suddenly vanished; unconsciously she drew back. "There's something else, Luke," she said. "Something far more important than a house. You said at Teal Lake that you didn't want children. Donald never wanted me to have a baby, either. But I want children. I always have."

He laced his fingers behind her back. "Maria, Ramon's youngest, took a shine to me as soon as she was old enough to smile. The last—"

"I can't imagine why," Katrin said.

"Stop interrupting. The last time I was there, I was lifting her high in the air and she was laughing fit to beat the band, and something shifted inside me. I realized I wanted to have children. But not just any children. Your children, Katrin. That if I never did that, I'd be a poor man for the rest of my days."

"If we have a little girl," Katrin said, her smile dazzling, "we could call her Maria."

"There's one slight hitch," Luke replied. "Here we are planning the kids' names, and you haven't actually said in so many words that you'll marry me."

"Serious oversight." She took his face in her palms, her features suffused with such tenderness that Luke felt his throat close. "Yes, Luke, I'll marry you. Because I love you with all my heart."

"I swear I'll never shut myself off from you again. Or leave you the way I did in Teal Lake."

"I believe you."

It was a vow, he thought, every bit as serious as the vows of marriage. Needing to lighten the atmosphere, he said, "I think we should dump some water on this fire, then go up to the tent and make love. Maybe I won't really believe any of this is real until I hold you in my arms. Besides, it's making love that makes babies, dearest Katrin. Or so I've been told."

"Great-aunt Gudrun said it was. And I never knew her to lie."

"Although if you've only got one sleeping bag, making love might be difficult."

She grabbed the pot of water that was sitting in the bushes, and threw its contents on the fire. The coals hissed, sending up a small cloud of ashes and smoke. "I also have two extra blankets. We can spread those under us, and use the sleeping bag on top."

"That's what I like. A resourceful woman."

"I aim to please," she said.

She led the way up the slope to the tent, where she crouched to unlace her hiking boots. Luke took off his shoes, crawling inside the tent behind her. She spread the blankets out while he unzippered her down bag. "It's cold," he said, tossing his jacket to one side and hauling off his shirt.

She gazed at his bare chest. "You mean I've got to take off all my clothes? I'm not sure Great-aunt Gudrun told me about that."

"Your courage is another quality I admire," Luke teased. "And I promise I'll keep you warm."

"I'll hold you to that," she said darkly, and pulled the fleece jacket over her head. Luke leaned forward, his fingers brushing her breasts as he unbuttoned her shirt. He wanted her so badly that he ached with need; as his eyes adjusted to the darkness, he saw the matching intensity in her face.

He stripped off the rest of his clothes, and drew her under the covers, her breasts soft and yielding against his chest. "Make love to me, Katrin," he said huskily. "Warm me, body and soul."

So she did. And afterward, as they lay naked in each other's arms, Luke knew himself to be the richest man in the world.

The world's bestselling romance series.

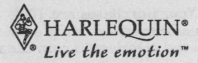

If you enjoyed what you just read,
then we've got an offer you can't resist!

Take 2 bestselling love stories FREE!
Plus get a FREE surprise gift!

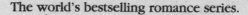

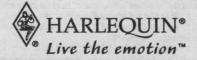

The world's bestselling romance series.

Seduction and Passion Guaranteed!

There are times in a man's life...
when only seduction will setttle old scores!

Pick up our exciting new series of revenge-filled romances—
they're recommended and red-hot!

Coming soon:
MISTRESS ON LOAN by Sara Craven
On sale August, #2338

THE MARRIAGE DEBT by Daphne Clair
On sale September, #2347

Available wherever Harlequin books are sold.

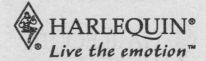

Visit us at www.eHarlequin.com